ANGEL EYES PUBLICATIONS
PRESENTS

More Birds More Bodies

J.D.B

J.D.B.

www.angeleyespublications.com

This is a work of fiction. The events and characters described herein are imaginary and not intended to refer to a specific place or living person. The opinions expressed in this manuscript are solely the opinions of the authors and do not represent the opinions or thoughts of the publisher.

All Right Reserved.
Copyright © 2020
Cover Design by Angel Eyes Publications

No portion of this book may be reproduced or utilized in any form or by any means cover design, electronic or mechanical, including photocopying, recording, or without prior permission in writing from the publisher.

ISBN-13:9781985675193

TABLE OF CONTENTS

Acknowledgements..5
Chapter 1..8
Chapter 2...22
Chapter 3...34
Chapter 4...41
Chapter 5...57
Chapter 6...72
Chapter 7...87
Chapter 8...97
Chapter 9..110
Chapter 10..129
Chapter 11..153
Chapter 12..181
Chapter 13..198
Chapter 14..209
Chapter 15..224
Chapter 16..238
Chapter 17..245
Chapter 18..255
Chapter 19..269

ACKNOWLEDGMENTS

This is for everybody who kicked rocks when the judge said, "Life." Don't get back on my dick now!!! What's smackin to my bro SMAMEZ LOC! Am I my brother's keeper? FRAZIER BOYZ! Eric and Elise. MOMMA DRAMA!

Homewood! Hale Street 300 block!!! What's smackin to the couple niggas left from the block. Boo-Loc, EeWee, D- Dub., Dare Dii, Catty Cat. Weezy. Dre, D-Dub Lit T.. Head, EJ, Big Ed and 8.

What's smackin to all my niggas upstate. I can't name everybody but y'all know Barry, Pinky, Barry, Tiger, Blasted, Tez, Skeddie, Ebo, SK, Soulja Reed, Ro, Diesle, Meez, Drama, Raw, Gizzle Bucc, Vga, J-Gutta, D-Ike, White Cuz, Bear, Bolo. Twiz, Mally, Fuck It, Ace, Mal D, Scoot, Tre, Junebug, Lil Ed, Eazy, Ray Ray, Lee Bug, Tadow, Chemical, Boogie, Pac, J-Bizz. Yayo, G-Shot, JB, Blue, Church, AV, Spark G, Lil Walt, Big J, Kalule, Pound, Chill, B-Dunc, and everybody else who's booked.

If I fuck with you I couldn't put everybody. Some niggas ain't on this list cause I found out yall some mufuckin rats. I guess the Chi-Chi wasn't cheesy enough?

Rest In Peace—Granny, Tee, Gangsta Roc, Lil D, Lil Ernie, Lil Russell, Sha Wag, P-Funk, Sherdina, Lil Ebony, Greedy, Sandy, Georgia, P-Jones, Octavia, Nut, Birdhead, Satyra and Lil Henry. And all the rest of the dead homiest!!

All of the women who influenced each female character. Y'all know who yall are. The 1 woman who had a major influence on all the characters—you probably thought I left you out, but you know who you are! Read between the lines babygirl. What's smacking?

This book is not based on true events or real people. It's all just a bunch of coincident! Just because a name is similar, or it might be your name doesn't mean that it's you. Alright, it is you—sue me!!!

Make sure yall get yall hands on my music as well. J.D.B. AKA J-Meanmug and 2501 Recordz present; Volume 1 Penitentiary Platinum"; "Volume 2 Penitentiary Diamond"; "Volume 3 Penitentiary Chancez (Head 1st)"; "40 Foot Wall (Tha Soundtrack)".

Check out my video live from the penitentiary for

my song, "Wutz Smackin 2Night". All of my niggas behinds bars should have my song, *"Jail Rich,"* on yall tablets.

Facebook.com/JMeanmug.Youtube.com/JMEANMUG

All my info is on Facebook. Hit me up. Start fucking with real niggas and leave them schmucks alone. Leave them rats alone. Yeah, he ain't tell on you.... Yet! Listen to my song, *"Rat Trap"* on the Limited Edition of Volume 3 Penitentiary Chancez (Head 1st).

Holla at me!

I ain't dead yet....

CHAPTER 1

"*I'm a stick up kid, that's how I live/I admit it/ I'm a stick-up kid, that's how I live/ and if ya doing too much, I'm coming to get it,*" Lyfe Jennings sang out of the stereo.

"Yo, cuz, I can't even think about hittin a lick without bangin this song first," I admitted to D-Slug, while he was taking the last hit of his green 50-quarter weed. I would listen to this song on repeat until I finished off a half pint of Vodka everytime we were getting ready to rob a nigga, and tonight was no different. It has become sort of a ritual. Me and D-Slug have been doing this for about 2½ months now.

I met Darnell, AKA D-Slug, in 2nd grade at Crescent Elementary school. I actually used to bully him, along with everybody else in the school. By the time that 1 was in the 6th grade, I was already in the game damn near headfirst because all of my niggas were at least 5 years older than me, so I had to jump in when they did. D-Slug is only a year younger than me, but he was not "off the porch" yet.

One day, me and my cousin, Lil Erny, was chilling on the block- the 300 block of Hale Street is one of the smallest streets in my hood. *It is only 4 blocks long but has 3 churches, I guess that's how many it takes to forgive us for just one day's worth of sins.* The 300 block is where the candy store used to be until somebody burned it down one night. Everyone thought that I was the culprit in that case. Now the block is just rundown row houses that brings more fiends to the block, which is known affectionately as "The Tre".

While me and Lil Erny were chilling, I saw D walking up our block. I immediately stood up to confront him, but Lil Erny grabbed me by my shoulders in order to stop me. Lil Erny was a short, cocky, nigga that could fight like a warrior.

"Why you grabbin me up, cuz?" I asked him while I was trying to get free from his trip.

"Cause, Darnell is our fuckin cousin," Lil Enry shot back like I should have known the answer.

"How?" I asked, not really wanting it to be true. Being family didn't mean that I couldn't beat him up, it just meant that Lil Enry would have to approve it. Lil Enry wasn't the Last Don or any boss type like that, he was just really into family sticking together at all times and looking out for each other instead of fighting each other.

"Our moms and his mom are cousins," Lil Enry responded. "Cathy, the one that got slumped by her nigga back in the day in front of the fire station."

I barely remember that because I was only like 5 years old when Cathy died, but I remember hearing my grandmother talk often about how cheating is an ultimate sin and that's why the reaper took her niece away.

"I still don't like that nigga though, " I said as he let me go.

Lil Erny called D-Slug across the street and told him to walk over to us, which D did hesitantly. Lil Erny saw the look on his face, I guess.

"Matter of fact, yall niggas gonna get a fair one right now. And you better fight back, Darnell," Lil Erny said like he was Don King.

Me and D-Slug fought for what seemed like an hour. It ended in a tie. Just a few bumps and bruises for the both of us.

A week later, me and the rest of the old Hale Street

niggas jumped D into the block. Me and D been right hands ever since. His family nickname was slugger, so we started calling him "D-Slug".

Oh, I almost forget, my name is Jakill Dujuan Freeman. Everybody calls me "JD" though. I'm 17 years old born on the 4th of July. I'm light skinned, 6 ft., 185 pounds *cut like a bag of dope*, and I have 17 tattoos. I grew up like everybody else in the worst section of Pittsburgh, Pennsylvania, known as the "Homewood" section due to all the homicides committed in my hood. The real name is Homewood though.

I been in and out of damn near every juvenile placement in PA and in a boot camp in Texas. My record goes from simple assault to an attempted homicide, which I beat but still had to do 9 months locked up for on GP. I always get out, start hustling, and within a month I would be locked up again for that or something else. I was never able to get a run at hustling. That's why I got into the stick-up game a couple months ago.

It was on my 17th birthday. Me and D-Slug wanted to go to the amusement park, Kennywood. There be tons of dimes with little shit on at Kennywood on 3 special days of the season. You have the Homiwood school picnic day. That's the day that all the bad ass hood bitches come out but us niggas always get into some gangsta shit before we can get on any of the dimes.

Another favorite day is the Penn Hills picnic day. It's not even a debate that Penn Hills has the overall sexiest broads in the city. I still have not seen an ugly Penn Hills woman. Then you have my birthday. That's when you will find all the baddest women in the entire county of Allegheny and all the outskirts of it. There be niggas from every hood, but we be so caught up with so many broads that we wait until the park closes before we start our bullshit.

This was one of those days to be there, but me and D- Slug only had enough for our small 35 grams of crack, pitch in, flip money. This was the first birthday that I made it out in time for and I was determined to make up for the ones that I missed. I refused to fuck up the flip though. Plus, we needed more money than that to live it up anyway.

While I was thinking about how we were going to get the money to stunt for the day, I saw the nigga, Tizz, walking up the alleyway.

Tizz was just a nigga that was copping off the nigga who was copping, but he had more money than us at that time. Tizz didn't play with guns and he couldn't fight. That nigga used to get beat up left and right. Skinny, little nigga with no headbusters in his entire family. Tizz was just your average 18-year-old hustler, but he was about to become your average 18-year-old victim.

It was one of those moments when the light turns green and you push the gas pedal all the way down without any thoughts about it.

As soon as Tizz walked on the side of the bushes near the intersection, where we had already shot out the streetlights, I pulled out my 38 snub and ran up behind him. D-Slug followed me without knowing what exactly I was about to do. I don't know how he didn't hear the determination in our footsteps, but it really would not have made a difference for him anyway.

"What's smackin, Tizz?" I asked once 1 got up close behind him.

Tizz spun around quickly, clearly scared as my

burner lined up with his nose. I swear you could see that nigga's heart pounding through his Polo shirt.

"What, what, what's this about, JD?" Tizz shuddered even though he already knew the answer.

"This bout whatever you got in ya pockets, nigga."

D caught on and went for Tizz's pockets. Tizz tensed up his body like he was thinking about trying to do something. I guess D sensed it too, because he looked up just as I smacked Tizz in his right eye with the small gun. He didn't drop, talk, or even move. He just stood there with tears falling down his face.

D finished going though, Tizz's pockets and grabbed a bundle of crack and 2 rolled up stacks of money. I smacked Tizz in the same eye again with my burner and told him to run.

The 2nd smack took all his fake gangsta right out of him. Tizz began running back down the alley like Carl Lewis, screaming about his eye.

D-Slug hollered to him, "Get some Clear Eyes! It gets the red out!" D-Slug always had something funny to say in any situation.

We couldn't stop laughing the entire way back to the spot. We got that lame for close to $800 apiece and 20 dubs of crack to put with our flip. That money was gone that same night after we hit the mall to get fly rented a fiends' car and went to Kennywood. We might have had a couple dollars left but we left Kennywood with 2 young dime bitches before the drama got crackin. You know the routine once we left the park.

The next day, while me and D were riding around in the "fiend buggie", we realized that it is a lot easier, and more fun to rob niggas than it is to hustle. It was at that very moment that our lives changed. Some might think it changed for the better, but some might think for the worst.

Now here we are, posted up at my mom's crib, getting ready to hit a lick. We had just robbed some weird motherfucker 3 days ago, but any stick-up kid will tell you that robbery money bums' holes in your pockets. You feel like you have to spend it A.S.A.P. You don't give a fuck about saving it because it really ain't yours.

We had pretty much stopped hustling because we didn't have time for it. We were too busy plotting and spending their money. This was one of those days when money starts to get low though, so it was time to hit another lick and get it smackin.

I had my mind made on jacking this older nigga, Spade. That nigga was holding a little bit of change. Other niggas were scared to rob him because a nigga tried it a couple years ago and ended up biting his own bullet after they tussled for the gun. Spade never even got arrested because for one time in history nobody snitched. Now Spade lives off that body, but if you knew anything about him, you would clearly be able to see that Spade is not killing a roach with Raid. You don't get any points for killing a nigga on some scared shit in my eyes.

Spade always hustles on Cora Street. Cora St. is the spot in the hood where everybody be just to stunt, get on bitches, or shoot dice. While I was down there a few times I noticed that he always goes in and out of the side cut that leads to my block. I instantly knew what was in that cut. He was going to find more than his stash in the cut tonight though.

I tossed D-Slug a mask once I finished my last shot of vodka. Tizz was the only nigga we ever robbed without a mask on.

"Play that song one more time before we roll, cuz. I

fuck with that one part, 'you ever seen a nigga diggin in the ashtray,'" D-Slug tried to sing.

"Yeah, that's what you call hard times and bad luck," I said as I grabbed a short out of the ashtray.

"Make sure we got everything," I said then lit the short.

"Mask and gloves, check."

We walked down the block until we reached the church parking lot that leads to the back Cora Street cut. Once D made sure that nobody was watching us, we crept down the small dirt hill and posted up in some thick bushes. We were on opposite sides though so that we could have Spade surrounded.

It's dark as fuck in that cut, so we didn't have to worry about somebody peeping us. The only thing in the back of Cora Street is the back doors to the row houses, stash spots, dried up blood, and broken bottles everywhere.

We almost jumped out of the bushes too early when Fiend Vita came strolling through. Luckily, we heard her screaming for her crackhead boyfriend, Shorty, before she walked all the way into the cut.

It was only about 15 minutes before Spade came walking into our trap. I knew that D heard sounds of broken glass being walked on, and the sound of Spade talking to himself.

"These niggas is sweet on the dice," Spade mumbled.

"Unless you want to find out how sour bullets is, don't move," I said as I jumped out of the bushes with my Glock 40 aimed at him.

D-Slug came from behind Spade without warning and hit him in the head a couple times with his rusty 45. That scared man shit tried to come out of Spade again because he attempted to wrestle with D for the burner. I didn't even have to do anything. D had Spade in the Full Nelson within 10 seconds. That bitch ass nigga started screaming for help. He must have forgot that if a nigga screams for help on Cora Street, ain't no niggas going to come running to save you because they'll be too busy getting in their cars and driving away.

I got all of Spade's money from his pockets and socks. That's when I noticed that this clown had a 380 in an ankle holster. He might be the only nigga in any hood with a fucking ankle holster, I thought as I put his 380 in my pocket and began taking all of his jewels.

"You can keep ya stash, so you can make some

more money for the next time we come through," D said and laughed.

We left Spade leaking as we dipped back the way we came but went to the cut crib on the block instead of my mom's crib.

The cut crib was my nigga, Big Hurt's mom's crib. She was always staying at her boyfriend's spot, so it was the cut crib by default. It wasn't nothing special though. Just a 2-floor duplex with a whole lot of extra furniture in it. I had bought a 20-inch TV off a fiend to put in the living room. It was good enough for the block niggas and a few broads to post up at while we're on the block.

Nobody was at the cut crib when me and D-Slug ran in the back door. We went straight to the dining room table as always. I put all the money and jewels on the table. It was worth the sticker bushes I got all over me, I thought after we split $7,238 down the middle.

"Cuz, that Jesus piece is fucking crazy. Jesus got bigger ice in his ear that I got in mine," I said while I was examining the 4-inch iced-out Jesus face hanging from one of the Cuban Links we took off Spade's neck. "We can't keep it though cause if I'd kill for it, I know he would kill for it."

"I ain't scared of no nigga," D responded and looked at me like I was crazy.

"I know that, D. But listen, when a nigga put change on ya head, you don't know who's coming to collect. Feel me?"

D took off the other Cuban with the iced-out money bag and sat it in the middle of the table with the 2 small canary pinky rings. "I dig that, cuz."

"You can keep all of the links. Just not the custom pieces. I still ain't rock that shit we took off Lil Face's neck," I said referring to the nigga we robbed 2 weeks ago about to get into his car in the Monroeville Mall parking lot.

"Just let me get that watch," I said while looking at the Jacob that D-Slug took off Spade's wrist and put on his own.

"You can have this. I'm a take Jesus to See Sonny for Money and see if he can take the ice out of it for me and he can keep the face," D-Slug replied. See Sonny for Money is the hood pawn shop that can make anything crack.

"So, what you bout to get into?" D asked.

"Kia," I responded with a smirk.

"What's ya plans, cuz?"

"Probably hit SQ. Then hit a freak," D said referring to Susquehanna St., the block that my older brother reps and where a lot of the freaks be at.

CHAPTER 2

Kia is a complete dime. Light skinned. Perfect 38 DD titties. Flat stomach, but not the starving look. Fat ass *not like Buffy's but close to it.* Sexy legs. 5 feet 4 inches and shoulder length hair. Lips that make you want to beg for some head. Face of a model. Hazel eyes. She's 19 years old and attends I.U.P. college in Indiana County (45 minutes from The Burgh). Kia got her head on straight and that completed her. But most importantly, her family got long money. If I ever be broke, I got a lick sitting right in front of me. I'm joking! Or am I?

I met Kia when me and D-Slug went to Kennywood on my birthday. She's not one of the broads that we left with though. I was standing in line at the Potato Patch to get some cheese fries. Directly in front of me in line stood Kia in the littlest shorts that she could squeeze that ass in and a flower-print bikini top. I knew right then and there that I had to get on her.

She ordered her food and when she got ready to pay for her order, that's when I quickly reached around her and gave the cashier $50 and told him to add my order to it.

"Thank you, but that don't mean that you're getting my number or anything else," Kia said with a tone that would have scared a schmuck away.

I looked her in her eyes with my game face on, ready for the obvious challenge. "Listen Pretty, if I would have thought that fitty ones would get me ya number, I would of just gave you a couple hunnit and said, 'let's roll'!" She shot me a crazy look like she couldn't believe that I said that to her so straight forward. Me not being intimidated, I continued, "I'm not gonna lie, you are physically sexy as hell, but I'm trying to get to know you mentally. Can I know ya name?"

"Kia," she said with a little giggle.

I swear that "get to know you mentally" shit never fails. Kia's playing hard to get went right out of the window.

We rode a few rides together, but we spent most of our time talking. Kia's conversation was way different than what I'm used to hearing where I'm from. It was her whole swag that stopped me from staring at her titties the entire time.

Honestly, I thought that Kia would be shook of me

once I told her that I'm from Homiwood, but it seemed like that intrigued her more. I knew that she had never fucked with a real G from the hood before by the way that she was fascinated, plus, she told me that she was from Stanton Heights. That's the "upper class" section of The Burgh where people have backyards, 2 car garages, and both parents at home.

Me and Kia chilled for a few hours and we were enjoying each other's company, but I knew that she wasn't trying to hit the Telly that night, and I saw D-Slug posted up by the Bumper Cars with 2 dimes. He was looking around like he was trying to find me, so I knew what it was hitting for. That's when I told my first lie to Kia.

"Damn Pretty, I wish I could post up with you longer but it's time for me to bounce," I said as I guided her away from view of D-Slug.

"What, you have a girl at home waiting for you?" Kia asked and giggled like she was joking.

"Naw, it ain't like that. I gotta pick up my grandma from the airport." I almost laughed when I said that because I couldn't think of another lie fast enough. It worked though.

"I hope that I made your birthday special, young

buck," she said when I gave her a hug.

If she was looking at my face when she made her "young buck" comment, she might have been scared to death. I don't know what it is about that word but I'm a grown ass man anyway.

Kia gave me a kiss on my cheek right before I made my escape to Freakville.

The very next day, Kia called me. We ended up talking for almost 3 hours about everything—honestly, she talked about everything and I just pretended to listen to it all.

Ever since that day, me and Kia talk on the phone every day before and after she studies. I also have been taking her out to different spots every weekend. That's how much I'm digging her. Before Kia, the only place that I was taking a woman to was to McDonald's and the Telly, and I wasn't even taking them to the Holiday Inn. All they got was the dirty ass Sunrise Inn with the roaches and cold water.

I'm definitely feeling Kia real heavy but the only thing killing it is the fact that I still have not fucked her yet. Don't get me wrong, I'm still running through hood hoes, but I think I'm ready to just kick it with Kia now.

I can't blame Kia for the reason why we still haven't got it in yet though. She had broken down and told me that she raped by her cousin when she was 14 years old at her grandmother's house and that's the only time that she "had sex." Therefore, she said that she wants us to wait until it feels right.

I think today is the day that Kia feels right about getting it crackin. She called me earlier today and asked me to drive out I.U.P. tonight because her roommate, Ashly, was staying at her boyfriend's spot. At first, I was thinking that she wanted us to just stay up all night and talk about the same shit that we have been talking about.

"Baby, I got a couple things I gotta handle tonight," I said, still debating on if I should drive up there or not. At least I wasn't lying. I had a hook-up planned with a little light skinned broad that was on my to do list for the past 2 weeks. Plus, me and D had to jack Spade.

"Please, Jakill, I have something special that I'm ready to give to you."

That pretty much translated to, "I want you to beat this pussy up!" Who am I to destroy mankind by not taking her up on her offer?

I don't even think I said bye before I hung up the phone and ran out of the crib. I went straight to Fiend Butch's crib and rented his Malibu for 2 days. He was my personal car connect. I think I drive his car more than he does.

After me and D left the cut crib, I headed straight to the liquor store in Wilkinsburg and grabbed a bottle of 151 Rum. I had to get right so that I could do the damn thang. I haven't smoked a Blunt in 4 years, but I could go for one right now, I thought. It would be perfect to enhance the Billy D swag for this occasion. I'll stick to the Rum, I decided.

I been drinking and driving for 20 minutes, with 20 more to go, and all I keep thinking about is who me and D are going to rob next. Them thoughts are fucking up my mood that I'm trying to get into, so I put in that old Donnell Jones CD.

"Tell me which way did she go/ Pretty young thang in the GS4" Donnell sang.

I'm glad that this smoker had some alright sounds in

the trunk because this song bangs and be having the hardest gangstas thinking about loving abroad.

I was so buzzed and tweaking that the rest of the drive felt like a blur. As I pulled into the Indiana University of Pennsylvania campus, all I saw was bad ass women everywhere. I think I might have saw maybe 5 niggas. I drove around for a minute just to take it all in. It was around 10:00 p.m. and it looked like people were just coming out. There was even a McDonald's and a Burger King on campus.

I followed the direction that most of the broads were heading in and came to a Sheetz gas station/store/club. It's not really a club, but it's definitely the spot. A couple of old school cars were parked with their sounds battling. Women were outnumbering the men 3-1. They were inside of the store and chilling in front shaking their asses.

I can't believe that I wasn't on to this spot a long time ago, but I will make sure that I see what it's hitting for if me and Kia don't work out.

After a half hour of sightseeing, I followed the directions to Kia's dorm that she gave me earlier. Since I knew her dorm room number, I walked through the dorm's front door behind somebody who got buzzed in so that I could surprise Kia.

I got off the elevator on the 8th floor and immediately saw broads walking through the hallway in shorts and bras. The dorm was broken down to women on the even floors and men on the odds, so I guess they felt comfortable. Or else they just don't give a fuck. Either way, I was at the right spot.

D-Slug would love this shit, I thought as a chocolate complexioned broad opened her dorm room door and made the music I heard louder.

"Oh, you must be Kia's man she kicked everybody out of her room for. Talkin bout 'don't any of yall come back till I'm done screamin'. Please put that girl out of her misery," the chocolate broad said and walked back into her room, ending the one-sided conversation.

At the end of the hall was room 814. Before I could knock, the door opened. I guess every woman in the building that saw me called Kia to let her know that I was there. It was either my natural hood swag or the clothes and ice I had on that let them know that I had to be who Kia was talking about.

Kia opened her door and I instantly knew that it was smackin tonight. She was standing there in some sexy red see-through lingerie that looked perfect on her skin. *Thank you, Vicky!* Her nipples were poking through the bra like they were trying to jump on me. As bad as I wanted to look down, I had to keep cool and not show her how bad I'm tweakin.

She even had some scented candles lit and Jagged Edge playing low in the background. There was no need for any words to be spoken.

I lifted her off her feet and started kissing her as I carried her to the bunk bed. I softly let her down right in front of it without stopping our kissing. I know that she felt my dick get hard as a brick while I held her close to me. My hands found their way to the hook on her bra and slowly took it off her while only breaking our kiss for a split second. I then began softly caressing her breast with my hands.

Kia licked my ear and whispered, "Be gentle and don't fuck me.... Make love to me."

That's all I needed to hear, I thought. I helped her step out of her panties and she began to undress me. We were both standing there completely naked taking each other in. I laid Kia down on the bottom bunk and went to work.

I started kissing and licking her neck and on down to her titties while she moaned from the feeling and the anticipation of what's sure to come. My right hand was making its way down past her belly button. Once my hand got to where her pubic hairs started, she closed her legs tight.

"Trust me, baby. I got you," I assured her.

Just like magic, her legs opened up again. I used my hand to slowly play with her clit. After a few minutes, I speeded up my hand's tempo as Ii licked down her stomach. As my tongue got close to her special spot, her body tensed until I reached it. Kia put her hands on my head and rubbed my waves while I licked and sucked on her swollen clit and slowly guided one finger into her tight pussy. She began squirming all over the bed and trying to rock her hips to my rhythm. I eased another finger inside of her and licked her clit even faster. The sound of Kia's moan made me enjoy pleasing her with lip and tongue service. She started screaming words that I couldn't understand until I hear, "Oh my God! You're making me cum!"

That was my cue. I came up slow, licking every inch along my way until I reached her lips. We passionately kissed again, letting her taste her own juices on my tongue. I slowly put my dick inside of her wet, but still extremely tight pussy. She instantly dug her nails in my back. I put her legs on my shoulders but had to take it easy on her. She screamed louder and louder with each deep stroke. Finally, we both came simultaneously.

The 151 that I was sipping on during the drive gave me the eye of the tiger though, so I kept "making love" to her the way she wanted it for a good 2 more hours. I came twice, and I lost count of hers.

I woke up naked to the sound of Kia singing Aaliyah's "One in a Million." An unfamiliar smile formed on my face when she looked at me.

"What are you smiling about this morning?" She asked while standing there in my boxers and wifebeater.

"I was thinking bout how I once heard that if you could make a woman cum and sing, you got her for life," I replied.

"Well, I'm definitely yours for life then."

We snuck into one of the female only showers and washed each other. Next thing you know, we were back at it like it never stopped the night before. I must have put it downright last night, I thought. I gave her a nice quickie while the shower rained down on us.

As soon as we started drying off, I remembered that I'm supposed to visit my older brother, Semaj ("S" as everybody calls him), this morning. Kia didn't want to let me leave, but I promised her that I'll take her out for the entire next weekend. She couldn't complain.

CHAPTER 3

I pulled up at SCI-Pittsburgh, better known as Western Penitentiary, around 11:00 a.m. Western Pen is a big gray-bricked castle looking pen. It looks exactly like the movies. The crazy thing is that it sits right on the last street of a fucking hood-Manchester. I'm still amazed at that. If you sit in Heinz Field, you can see the pen from there.

I was glad that I made it into the visit room before count so that I wouldn't have to wait until 1:00 p.m. to visit S.

The first things that I did, as always while I wait for S to come, was looking to see if there are any broads in the visit room worth taking to the Telly after they get done lying to their niggas about being faithful. There was one or two worthy of my attention, but I'll focus on that later.

I only had to wait a few minutes before S came walking out of the "inmates only" door looking just like an older version of me. I could see that something was wrong by the look on his face. S is a crazy but quiet nigga, so there is no telling what is on his mind.

"What's smakin, bro?" I asked like I couldn't pick up on the vibe.

As always, he got right to the point. "I been hearing bout you and lil D-Slug out there going crazy. Niggas say y'all got mufuckas noid to come out they crib with more than a buck on em," S said seriously.

"How the fuck niggas in here know it's me and D?" I asked confused as we walked to some open seats far away from the COs.

"Nigga, we know shit before niggas on the streets know shit cause we got nothing but time to listen. Ya dig?"

"Yeah though, I'm putting a stack on ya books when I bounce, and I'll give you another stack in a few days," I said trying to change the subject.

"That's cool, but I want to holla at you bout the way you goin bout ya hustle. I know you don't like taking advice and you ya own man, but jackin was my shit so you should learn from me," S said in a serious tone.

Some dirty bitch's son started screaming for a bag of chips from the vending machine, but I knew off top that ol' girl was flat broke. I was thinking about giving him some of the $30 worth of tokens that I got from the front lobby on my way in, but he started banging and kicking on the machine. That got their visit terminated right then and there.

"Want to grab some food?" I asked still attempting to change the subject even though I know that once S has something to say, he won't stop until he finishes.

"Naw, not yet. You listening to what I'm saying?"

"I'm with you, bro."

"You are getting a couple dollars, but you ain't getting no money. Dig me? Y'all jackin niggas while they're on the street for a couple dollars, but all the money is in their cribs, cuz. Niggas got safes filled with cheddar and blow. If you run down on a couple of the right niggas and get, they safes, y'all I be up and not jackin mufuckas no more. Y'all I be slangin they work back to em," S said and paused for a second to make sure that I was following him, then continued, "Don't risk ya life for a nigga's pockets, cuz. I know you'll bust ya gun too, but you know how the game go. And when I get out in a couple years, I'm try in to be able to stomp with you. Not visit you in the joint or at the cemetery, bro. Ya dig? Get you a crib in the cut somewhere and a car with ya money. Just make sure you plan ya shit out perfectly and have lil D-Slug on the same page.

"The number one rule is if a nigga moves shoot him. Cause when niggas is faced with death, they'll try to do anything with their last breath to stay alive or take you with em. Get that money lil bro and stay safe," S finished and got quiet for a minute to make sure his teachings sunk in.

I sat there breaking down everything that S just said to me because it made more than sense, it made dollars.

We went on and talked about back in the day, old hoes, new hoes, who's rats, and whatever else came to mind while we ate microwaved buffalo wings, bacon burgers, and some type of strawberry shortcake that was better than homemade strawberry shortcake. After taking flicks with other Homiwood niggas that was on visits at the same time as us, I gave my older brother a hug and rolled. I put $1,000 on his books and walked to my car looking at the flicks of niggas with the regular penitentiary poses. I'll put these on the wall in the cut crib with the rest of them to keep niggas names ringing, I thought. Then I began thinking about how it's been so long since me and S was home at the same time.

S been locked up on this trip for 3 years already but been in and out since he was 11 years old—he'll be 20 in a couple of months. He had got certified as an adult for a couple of guns and some work.

S and his nigga, Half, was in their trap house when the pigs ran in and found the shit. As soon as the handcuffs hit their wrists, Half snitched that everything that the pigs found were S's. Initially S got sentenced to 6½-21 years upstate, but he came back on his appeal and ended up with 6-12 years to do.

Before S got grabbed on that case we were only home together for a month, but I was on house arrest and he was on the run for an attempted homicide, so we only got to post up with each other for maybe a half hour a day.

The attempted homicide that S was on the run from had the pigs watching me to find him. They acted like it was something major.

Some nigga shot S in his leg as he walked out of the store on Brushton Ave. The nigga tried to run and ended up catching a couple of 9 bullets in his back. S managed to limp away but the other nigga was fucked up. The pigs came and questioned ol boy while he was laying there bleeding to death, stopping the ambulance from helping him. If the pigs would have held up the ambulance any longer ol boy would have died and not been able to snitch once he got to the hospital like he did.

S waited a couple of hours before he went to St. Francis Hospital, but the pigs must have put the word out at all hospitals in The Burgh. S noticed the doctor acting strange, so, S being S, he punched the doctor, dropped him, and limped out of the hospital before the pigs could get there. He laid low until it was time to ride on a nigga or hit a lick. All his licks used to end up with somebody getting shot, so it was like he was ridin anyway.

S never found the nigga he shot before he got booked with half, so I was on the hunt for him while the house arrest people thought that I was at school. One day I went to my duck off spot. That was my little freak, Erica's crib. The door was unlocked as usual and as I walked in the house, I couldn't believe ol boy was sitting right there on her couch. I quickly pulled out my little 22 revolver and that nigga started acting like 1 had a fucking rocket launcher.

"Please don't kill me, JD! Homies, I ain't goin to court!" He screamed.

I find it funny how niggas will lie on anything—

even their dead "homies" but expect you to believe them.

I couldn't kill him right there though, unless I slumped Erica too, and that would have been a waste of good pussy and an ultimate mess. So, I told the nigga that I would be standing in front of the courthouse and if I saw him, I was going to kill him right there. Then I patted him down and found a pretty ass blue steel Jennings 9mm with a beam on it. I couldn't believe that he had a Nina on him and didn't try me with this small, rusty 22. I still laugh about that to this day. I took his burner and a couple hundred dollars out of his pockets, then dipped. Erica stood there the entire time loving the action. *He wouldn't be fucking her today,* I thought.

I swear now that I think about it, that nigga reminded me of the nigga on Belly in the spot after they hit that lick in the beginning of the movie.

I don't know if it was me or his conscience, but the nigga ain't come to court on S, so they threw that case out.

I wanted to kill the nigga, Half, bad but S made everybody let him breathe because that was personal, and he wanted to handle that himself when he got out.

CHAPTER 4

I snapped back into today when my cell phone came to life with the new J-MEANMUG ringtone for his song *"Wutz Smackin 2Night."*

"Yo?" I answered.

"Where you at, cuz, still with ya future B.M., Kia?" D-Slug asked and laughed.

"I just came from postin with S for a minute. He said what's smackin. But listen, we were rappin bout some real shit I gotta holla at you bout but we'll rap in person. What you get into last night though?"

It was like D had a sexcapades lined up with a new freak every single night. To be a skinny midnight completed nigga, I got to give him his props. I was waiting for him to give me details so I could decide if the broad was worth me knocking off too.

"You won't believe I ain't get no pussy last night," he replied and almost made me crash into the back of a Neon.

"What is you trying to go for that new 'born again'

virgin look?" I joked and we both laughed.

"No, cuz, listen, I hooked up with Tiff and Shalynda. Yo, I took them to the Telly and them hoes started kissing and shit before I even sat down. I mean they was goin crazy, sucking titties, licking pussies, grindin, and all that shit, JD. So, I sat back, lit up some dro and watched the show." D said excitedly.

Tiff and Shalynda…. Tiff and Shalynda been on my to do together list for a minute now. I used to fuck with Tiff and Shalynda at one point when they were only into niggas but me being a jailbird fucked that up before I got the chance to fuck either of them. They both are dimes. Tiff is about 5' 4", light brown skin, thin with a little bubble on her back. Shalynda is about 5'7", pale light skin, and just a little thick with sexy ass lips.

D-Slug know how I'm tweakin for both of them, so I know he went at them just to have something to talk shit about. That was our game we played so I couldn't look at him sideways for it. I got him a handful of times.

"You mean to tell me you had two sexy lil bitches at the Telly kissing and licking each other and you just sat back smoking.

What the fuck kind of dro was that, cuz?" I asked,

still grinding him up for not knocking off 2 of the sexiest freaks in the hood.

"Cuz, I was tweakin to fuck both of em, but I didn't want to fuck it up. This was my first time seeing some shit like that in person. I had to play it, how it goes, and guess what, nigga." D asked but quickly continued without letting me respond, "Yeah, when we left the Telly, they told me to pick them back up tonight for a ménage."

I couldn't believe what I had just heard but instead of feeling some type of way because my right-hand man is going to get those stripes before me, I just tried to blend on the session. "Oh, I'm rolling with you, cuz."

He quickly shot me down. "Not at all. I got to reap from what I sowed first, but, homies, I got you next time. What happened with Kia last night? You ain't get no pussy either, huh?" D-Slug asked as if he was sure.

Now it's my turn to stunt, I thought.

"Yo, it finally went down last night. We were on some real-life movie shit; D. Kia had the whole spot set up and the Vicky's on. I'm telling you, I put in all that time with her for a reason. She's special, cuz." I replied with too much Leon shit.

D-Slug started laughing so hard that I could hear his

lungs grasping for air that wasn't there. All he kept saying was, wait till S hear this shit and this nigga's crazy!"

I knew where this conversation was headed now that I had put my foot in my mouth, so I told him to meet me at the cut crib on the block in an hour. Then I hung up while he was trying to get another joke in.

Instead of driving straight to the block I decided to get my hair cut, so I drove to Willy T's on the Ave.

Willy T's was the type of hood barber shop that movies be trying to make their shit look like. I'm not saying that Homiwood had the only real hood barber shop, because I can think of a perfect example on the Northside of The Burgh. When you walk in Willy T's though, it looks more like a fuckin club.

After I parked my fiend buggie in the KFC parking lot, I walked into Club Willy's. It was the usual in there. There were niggas playing pool in the side room and women chillin towards the back of the spot, gossiping about the niggas in the side room probably. Little bad ass hood kids running around getting on everybody's nerves, so people started giving them money in hopes that that would calm them down.

Only 4 barbers were there, and as usual Chris had a

MORE BIRDS MORE BODIES

gang of mother fuckers waiting to get into his chair. Chris is one of those barbers that can do absolutely anything to your head that you ask him to. If you want a fade—he can do that. It don't matter if you want a fucking Statue of Liberty designed out of your afro—he can do that.

Being that me and Chris is cool, due to the fact that I been sitting in his chair since I was around 10 years old, he pushed his line back a spot for me like he always does. Chris told everybody that I was already next. There was a little bit of mumbling, but I don't give a fuck. I had to wait until he finished giving a boy a shape-up.

Within 5 minutes of walking into the spot I was sitting in Chris' chair.

"What's smackin, cuz? You already know how I rock it. What's new, nigga? What up?" I asked like I really cared that much.

"You, nigga. That's what's up. The word down here is that the nigga, Spade, is on you and Slug's heels. I know you strapped though," Chris said in his own form of gossiping, hoping that I would help him become the first person in the shop with the real word of mouth scoop on the situation.

"Hell, yeah I'm strapped, nigga," I lied.

I can't believe that I forgot to pick up my burner, I thought. I had to drop it off on the block before I went to visit my brother because sometimes them punk ass COs want to play Task Force and check a nigga's car in the parking lot. *Damn I'm slipping,* I thought.

"And you already know I'm quick to use it. I don't know what the beef with Spade's bout though." I added.

Chris ain't go for that bullshit and he was still trying to dig. "Nigga. quit frontin. Everybody in here know yall got him down Corma. Y'all the only two niggas jackin everybody in sight."

I'm surprised that he didn't nick my head the way I leaned up so fast after his response. I turned around and gave him that I-kill-you-if-you-say-that-shit-again look. Then I leaned back and finished getting my hair cut without any further conversation.

As soon as my fresh cut was complete, I gave Christ $20 and told him good look on the heads up.

"You still my nigga," Chris said as I left.

I was walking across the street to the parking lot when I felt that something was wrong. You can say that it was my "Spider Sense". I turned around just in time to see.

Spade's white, bubble-back, SS Monte Carlo driving

slowly through the lot. I hurried and jumped in the fiend buggie just as he let off 2 punk ass shots. Then he sped away like he thought that he shot me. I guess that was a front, because Spade had to be duck hunting due to the fact that not me or the car had any bullet holes.

I drove to the cut crib thinking about a million different ways to kill Spade. I walked into the spot and was instantly hit by a cloud of dro smoke. D-Slug was at the beginning of the smoke. D and Daz was playing 007 on the Nintendo 64 while E-Wok, Boo, and Big Hurt was sitting on the run-down couches smoking.

In total, my block is 9 niggas deep, but you know how inside of every squad there's a usually a couple of circles. My circle is just me and D-Slug ever since Lil Erny and the older niggas started posting up on Fleury Way.

The Tre is me, D-Slug, Boo, E-Wok, Daz, Big Hurt, Teeke, Mayo, and Gizzle. Boo is the quiet one. He's always thinking and paying attention to everything. A 5'10" brown skin nigga with puffy eyes. Boo was the only one, besides me, that didn't fuck up his money. His only problem was that he didn't have that much money to fuck up.

E-Wok is one of those niggas that nobody knows how he became part of the squad or when. It's like he been there for a while, but you know that it ain't been that long. E-Wok, or Wokky as we sometimes call him, is the brokest from the block. It didn't help that he was 5'4", skinny, and black as fuck. He was also becoming the nigga that we were blending away from whenever he came around.

Teeke is the nigga that don't give a fuck about anything but the block. His mom and younger brother died when their house went up in flames during one of his mom's get high or die trying routines. Teeke had just happened to be at the cut crib that night. Me and Teeke could pass as brothers, as far as looks. We're the same height, weight, and complexion. We even have the same facial features. The only differences are that Teeke has green eyes and long braids, that he wore in 6 braids to the back at all times.

Daz is the youngest at only 14 years old. I try to keep him out of shit, but he does everything he sees someone else do. The only good thing is that he makes sure he goes to school on the regular. Daz sort of resembles Jay-Z, with that whole camel look. He's the second tallest nigga from the block at 6'2", but he didn't play any sports.

Mayo was the tallest. 6'5" and about 210-lbs cut up. He was the star point guard on Westinghouse's basketball team 3 years ago that won the state championship his senior year. He even got invited as an All American to play in the McDonald's game. Mayo was going to be a beast in the pros, as he already secretly planned to do only one year at Pitt, where he already had committed to go. He was going to make The Tre known worldwide and put us where we deserved to be. But like everything else gold in the hood, it turns to shit very quickly. During a pick-up game at Mellon Park, Mayo accidently fouled a nigga in his face and the nigga didn't care that Mayo apologized for it to let him know that it was an accident. The nigga ran to his duffle bag, pulled out a 45 and shot Mayo once in his back and once in his left knee. That nigga died 2 days later (I plead the 5th) but that didn't make Mayo feel any better. He would never be able to play ball again. What made it worse was the fact that all of this took place 1½ weeks before the McDonald game. That's why he's still on the block and has a chip on his shoulder.

Big Hurt is 6'1" but 375 lbs. A Biggie Smalls

looking nigga. He ain't a hustla or a gangsta. On top of that, he doesn't like to fight. He'll try certain motherfuckers though. He was a cool nigga, but if it wasn't for his mom's crib, I don't think he would be from the block.

Gizzle is Mayo's youngest cousin but they act nothing alike. Gizzle is a live wire and you never know what he's going to do until he does it. He's a brown skin, 5'10", thin nigga with a 'me against the world' complex. He also might be the only nigga from The Tre that could out smoke D-Slug.

Don't get me wrong, I'll ride or die for the entire squad, but when it comes to trying to get money, me and D are the only ones making it happen.

So naturally we blend off from them, and since we ain't hustling any more, we only post up with them a couple days out of the week.

"What's smackin, niggas?" I asked.

Everybody just nodded at me like they were in the ultimate zone.

Boo slowly looked up. "Ain't shit, cuz, but when you gonna put me on a couple of those licks you and D be hittin?" He asked.

"I got you. Soon as we make this move, me and D

trying to put all the niggas on," I said thinking about how Boo is probably the only one of them, besides D-Slug, who really has that hunger to get money.

I waited for one of the Bonds to kill the other. "Slug let me holla at you out back real quick," I said to D-Slug, who, from the look on his face, was clearly the James Bond that got slumped.

D hesitantly got up. "It better be important. Fuckin up my high, and that nigga might try to bounce without lettin me win my money back," D-Slug said as we headed to the back door.

"The nigga, Spade, just clapped at me, cuz," I said as soon as the door closed behind us.

"The nigga knows we got him. Soon as I came out Willy T's, he caught me slippin. Bust two shots and ain't hit shit. The crazy thing is Chris was just tellin me that ol boy was on our tops while he was cuttin my hair."

"I know you busted back," D said as he pulled out his burner and looked at it.

"Nigga, I forgot to grab my burner after I visited S."

D-Slug just shook his head knowing that might have been the only time that I have ever been anywhere without my heat on me.

"So, we gonna catch him down Cora or what?" D finally broke the moment of silence.

"Naw, cuz. We gonna catch him at his crib and kill two birds with one stone. That's what else I got to holla at you bout. S got me thinkin right," I said and put him on to the conversation that me and my brother had.

After I finished relaying S's entire speech, D finally spoke again. "Yeah, I feel that, JD. But when we get up, I'm definitely gonna miss this stick-up kid shit," D-Slug said, then paused for a second like he was going down robbery memory lane.

"Fuck it though. Let's get this paper. So, I guess Spade is up first?"

"No doubt about it. In a couple days we gonna lay on his crib and catch him goin in. Then we gettin him and whoever with him. I'm killin him off top."

"That's one thing for sure and two things for certain," D replied.

"I'm bout to hit the crib and change up. I think I'm a go knock off one of the Avenue bitches after I take Butch's ride back," I said as we began to walk through the side cut to the front of the cut crib.

"I got Daz's mom's ride for the whole week and I

only gave her a buck. I'll be pushing the Grand Am till next Saturday, cuz."

Daz's mom, Ms. Pumkin, is the only smoker I know with 3 new cars, and a good job at Blue Cross. I guess she rather rent out a car that she ain't drivin than to spend money to get high. The funny thing about it is that she won't let Daz drive any of them because she says that 'he ain't responsible.' I swear you'll hear the craziest shit in the hood.

D continued, "Yeah, and I got that ménage supposed to be smackin tonight. I'm bout to grab a Telly and hide some cameras in that bitch so I can get it all on tape. I might fuck around and slang that shit on Ebay or something," D said and started laughing.

"Hood Hoes Gone Wild," I added.

"Just make sure I'm included in the next go round."

We pounded each other up, then dipped off in different directions, leaving nothing but tire smoke.

After I got out of the shower, I was getting dressed and started thinking about Kia. I haven't called her all day, but I had to call Lil Erny first.

"Who this?" Lil Erny asked into the phone.

"It's JD, nigga. Like you ain't look at the Caller ID before you answered with that noid shit, cuz. What's the haps with those big thangs? That's what I wanna know?" I said, referring to some Chopprs-AK 47 he was selling.

Lil Erny had become the hood gun connect for the past year. I don't know how he stumbled across them, but I know that as long as he had guns and the hood had drugs, he would never go broke. A nigga in the game can never have enough guns. Not only that, guns get bigger and better every year. That's why I'm trying to get my hands on these Choppers.

"Everything's everything, lil cuz. I kind of figured you'd be callin me bout them once I heard bout the situation with dude. Them lil mufuckas yall be dumpin with is for beefin with yaself. Dig me? How many you try in to grab though?"

"I need three just in case I gotta toss one."

"Stack me up. and I got something extra for you too!" Lil Erny said, letting me know that it's going to run me a stack-$1,000.

That has to be the family discount, so I ain't going

to try to get him lower than that, I thought.

"Aight. I'll swing through Fleury in a minute. Be ready for me, cuz," I said as I ended the conversation.

I immediately called Kia before I make her think that I'm dodging her. "Kia, what's up, baby? My bad I ain't hit you back earlier but I had to take care of something after I saw S. How you feelin though?" I asked.

"I'm feeling good now that you called," Kia said in a tone that something was on her mind.

"Baby, you got my cell number," I responded, not trying to pry.

I heard her take a deep breath.

"I wanted to call you, but I also wanted to wait until you called me, because I really don't know where we stand after ...." Kia broke off her sentence, allowing me to put it together myself, then she continued, "You know. It's hard to explain."

"Kia, listen, I understand what you mean three hunnit percent, but you gotta understand that every nigga ain't foul. I'm sorry bout what happened to you and I know you'll never forget that, but what happened last night was special. You gave me something special and I love you for that and for many other reasons. Nothing bad will ever happen to you again because you are my woman. Feel me?" I said with all sincerity.

She didn't respond, but sat quiet for a minute, probably thinking about the same thing that I was thinking about.

That was the first time that I ever said those 3 little words to any woman who wasn't my family and actually meant it.

After a long minute of silence, which felt like an hour, Kia softly said, "I love you too, JD."

We bullshitted on the phone for about an hour. I had to pick up Lil Erny and my new burners, so I was happy as fuck when Kia said that she had to study so she'll call me back later or tomorrow.

CHAPTER 5

"These mufuckas is pretty as fuck, cuz," I said excitedly while examining the Choppers.

"And ain't no bodies on em, nigga. No dirt at all." Lil Erny said with his used-car dealer pitch as he sat in the passenger seat holding a bag full of who-knows-what.

"Cuz, stop the bullshit. I'm coppin em even if they had ten bodies on em. All I'm a do is add to the count anyway." I tossed Lil Erny a rubberbanded stack of bills and started the car back up.

"Oh yeah, what else you got for me?" I asked curiously.

Lil Erny reached into his bag. "Here, lil nigga," he said and handed me (2) 75 round drums for the Choppers, and 4 boxes of bullets, to go with the 3 banana clips he had already given me.

"Good fuckin look, cuz," I said even more excited than I was.

"I figured you'd need more slugs since you probably still can't aim for shit," he said and started laughing, referring to my attempted homicide.

Aight look, I didn't want to mention it, as you have probably noticed, but I might as well.

I was 13 years old. Me and a few of the Hale Street niggas, including Lil Erny and D-Slug, was posted up at our old cut crib on the corner of Hale St. and Hamilton Ave. We were all smoking some regular dirt weed, like everybody else at that time, when me and this nigga, Black, from the squad started arguing about who the blunt was supposed to get passed to next.

What niggas don't know was that I was waiting on a reason to air Black out. Black was a Black ass weird motherfucker. He used to just say dumb shit out of his mouth for no reason at all. Plus, he was 4 years older than me and every now and then he would attempt to treat me like his young nigga around some hoes to make himself look like an oldhead or something. I always cut that short as soon as he tried it, but it was always stuck in the back of my mind. So pretty much, I was just waiting on a reason.

While we were arguing Black said one too many

cuss words. I pushed him over the coffee table and unloaded all 17 shots, while I was standing only about 3 feet away from him. Everybody except Black's right hand man, Dre, ran out of the crib and left them there. We all thought for sure that Black was dead.

To our surprise Black survived and kept his mouth closed. However, that gay ass nigga, Dre, told on me as soon as the police walked into the crib. Way before court, Dre was found shot and burned up in a stolen car inside of the bowling alley's parking lot.

You're probably wondering how Black survived 17 shots. That's why I didn't want to mention this shit. Out of 17 shots at close range—and I was gunning for his head—I only hit the nigga once in his fucking lung. I felt dumb as fuck! And as you can see, niggas still clown about that till this day, but only niggas that I'm close to.

Anybody else will see how much my aim improved. That's also the last time that I ever smoked.

I dropped off Lil Erny at the corner of Fleury and Sterrett Street where a gang of other hood niggas were hustling. Then I drove straight to the cut crib and put 2 of the Choppers in my stashspot in the basement, which was an old half of bathroom that been out of order and boarded up since Big Hurt's mom moved into the crib.

I spent the next 10 minutes or so listening to 2Pac and loading up a drum while nobody else was there for once. I don't know what it is about AK47s that make a nigga want to kill somebody right then and there, but I began trying to remember if anybody owes me money or if I still have other unresolved beef with anybody else besides Spade. It's similar to how the car Christine was in that old movie.

After realizing that I didn't really have any other beef to go on a rampage about, I put a Chopper in the trunk and drove over to Butch's spot. Butch was sitting on his porch with Vita and Shorty, probably talking Vita into tricking for some work. Whoever tricks with her should just shoot their self, I thought as Butch walked to the car when he noticed that I wasn't getting out of the car.

"Yo, I need the ride for two more days," I said and put $100 in his hand, so he couldn't resist temptation.

"That's cool, lil nigga. I needed that bad," Butch said then continued, "but why don't you just buy ya own shit as much as you rent mine?"

"I been thinkin bout that. I got my license when I was booked, but I can't put a ride in my name, and my mom definitely ain't putting it in hers," I said thinking about how me and my mom really ain't that cool right now.

My mom feels some type of way about the dirt I be in constantly and all of the "blood money" and drugs and shit of that nature that I bring into her house. The crazy thing is that after my dad left when I was one years old, she started fucking with the 'that Nigga' of that age group. She was the O.G. broad of the hood, but then one day out of the blue, a couple years ago, she did the whole born again Christian thing and began looking at me like I was Satan in the flesh. That's the reason that I only go there while she's at work or already sleep.

"Lil nigga, I'll put it in my name for five hunnit," Butch said with his eyes wide.

The number one rule of negotiation is to shoot high off top.

"Naw, but I'm sure you'll do it for three."

"Deal! When you want to handle that?" Butch asked excitedly, which made Vita stood up so she could try to figure out what was going on.

"I'm a bring ya ride back Tuesday morning and

we'll shoot to the spot then. I'm letting you know now, Butch, if you try to report," I was saying until Butch cut me off.

"JD, I'm a crackhead, not an idiot," he said clearly feeling disrespected. "I knew you since you were a pup, lil nigga, so I know what ya capable of. It would be nice if you still toss me something every now and then."

"I'm still gonna look out, and I'll send Boo at you. You can trust my nigga, Boo, with ya ride," I said as I put the car in drive.

"I'll see you Tuesday," he screamed as I drove away.

I drove to the row houses on the Ave. by Baxter Park and hopped out. It was the usual suspects there-Keva and her gang of bitches, and Drizzy and his gang of niggas.

"What's smackin, niggas?" I asked and pounded up most of the niggas and hugged a few bitches.

"What's new with you, cuz?" Drizzy responded.

Drizzy is a Fleury Way nigga. All he does is get drunk all day and sell a couple dubs. I met him through Lil Erny a minute ago. Me and Drizzy is cool and all but I'm mad as fuck that he is up there right now because Keva is his broad.

Keva is light skinned, about 5'7", 145 lbs. She has the perfect body—even after she had her daughter. Pooh. Fat ass. Thighs. Titties. All that shit, plus she's pretty in the face. Keva is a regular hood bitch, but me and her have a little history. We were fucking for a while until she got knocked up and Drizzy wifed her. The whole time Drizzy and this nigga from Lincoln, Lazy, was beefing over her, I was busting nuts all up in her. He still doesn't know that I was knocking her off, even though I had her first. Don't ask don't tell.

Recently there has been flirtations between me and Keva again, so I been trying to catch her alone but Drizzy never uncuffs her. I can understand why a little bit though—the same reason why I'm here right now for her. Keva got that fire pussy. That shit is wet, fat, tight, warm, and anything else that puts good pussy into the good pussy column. She even throws it back at you. I mean that shit will have you busting in less than a minute. I swear to God! We had to have fucked at least 500 times, and I never even tried to get any head from her. That's how good her pussy and fuck game is.

Drizzy had the nigga, Dirty Mike, with him as usual. This dirty motherfucker is the world's number 1 hater!

He's one of those miserable niggas that ain't got shit and instead of trying to get shit, he rather just talk shit. His hating is different though because he always knows somebody to compare a nigga to. You can pull up in the hardest Grand National and he would say something like, "That's probably just a regular kitted Regal. I know a nigga with a real Grand National." Females ain't exempt either. A broad could walk past with a fat ass that have niggas going crazy. This nigga would be like, 'Cuz, her ass ain't shit. It's her jeans making her ass look like that. I know a bitch with a perfect ass.' That shit be entertaining for a minute, but it turns annoying quick. You be ready to slump him about him hating on somebody else's shit. Trust me, I was close to it a couple times."

I knew that I wasn't going to be able to get it smackin with Keva, so I blended off and sat on the steps with Laneisha.

Laneisha is a creamy chocolate complexion. 5'10", about 120-lbs at the most. She has a thin body, but she still has a bubble ass. Handful size titties, but they're just right for her frame. Long hair, but she still be putting weave in it every now and then. Baby girl is definitely sexy though. What tops it off is that Laneisha is 16 years old and the last virgin in the hood. We done damn near everything but fucked. She even had that little attitude that have niggas, besides me, shook.

The only thing wrong with Laneisha is that I can tell that she's not capable of riding out with a nigga if he gets booked. She is the type that need somebody right there to chill with. You know how some broads just get lonely quick? She strikes me as that type. I take too many penitentiary chances to invest in that. I learned that lesson already. Don't get me wrong though, she's the perfect woman if you're not in the game. Me being a gangsta, it would never work.

So, I just post up with her and try to hit every now and then. I look out for her too because besides not being a rider, baby girl is thorough—if that makes any sense.

"What's smackin, sexy? Why you actin like you ain't know I was coming over here?" I asked Laneisha.

"I just thought you was going to find a way to slide off with Keva."

She cut her eyes at me then continued, "Don't think that everybody's slow as Drizzy is. I just can't figure out why you're always around me instead."

"Come on, Neisha Boo," I said calling her by the

nickname that I gave her. "We both know why I'm always around you. I been diggin you since I met you two years ago."

"Well, why ain't you try to holla at me back then." She asked curiously.

"Cause you know how ignorant you be. I ain't want you to play me." I admitted.

She gave me a sinister smile. "I wouldn't have played you, Jakill. I used to walk down Hale Street every day for no reason at all but to just try to get your attention," Laneisha explained and shyly looked away from me. "Why you ain't try to be my man recently as much time we spend together?"

I had to think of the right words to put it in so that I wouldn't ruin any chances that I might have had.

"I'm a keep it all the way funky with you. I would love to be ya man, and if I wasn't into the things that I'm into, I would make that happen ASAP. But right now, all it would lead to is me hurting you and you hurting me. I care about you enough to not hurt you. Feel me?" I responded.

Laneisha didn't say a word. She just stood up, grabbed my hand, and led me up the steps into her mom's row house.

Usually, we would come inside, kiss, lick, and all the warmup shit. Then she would stop me from trying to put my dick inside of her. I would then be mad as fuck but act like I'm cool so that I might get another shot. It had become a sort of game, a challenge. I got the feeling that the challenge is over tonight.

We walked through the hallway and into Laneisha's room. Not trying to play myself, I stood at the doorway while she turned on Tyrese's *"Sweet Lady"* on her radio that I bought her for her birthday. That gave me the green light to walk over to her with timed steps and put my lips on hers. We began to kiss heavy, and at the same time we were taking each other's clothes off until we stood in each other's embrace completely naked.

The smell of her peach body spray was making me tweak even more. I laid her down on her bed slowly. Her breathing was heavy, and my dick was hard, both from anticipation. I had already made up my mind that I wasn't going to eat her pussy tonight, because I refuse to get my face smutted and then told to stop when I try to hit.... like last time. I began sucking on her titties and licking around her hard nipples. Her hands were rubbing up and down my back and shoulders. As soon as I opened her legs all the way, she asked me, "Do you have a condom?"

"No," I lied. "Don't worry, baby, I'll pull it out." I lied again.

Why do all of us niggas use that line? "Just let me put the head in."

I guess she was comfortable with that answer or else she knew that I was lying, and she knew it.

It took me 15 minutes to finally get my dick inside of her virgin pussy. She was wet as fuck and extremely tight to the point that I had to think about something else so that I wouldn't bust off top. Laneisha squeezed her legs around me as tight as she could while I slow stroked her. I can tell that she can't take the dick, so I didn't even bother to put her legs on my shoulders. She probably would have yanked them back down immediately. Once she dug her nails into my back, I began to speed up the pace a little bit, which caused the sound of her moans to amplify.

"Oh, Jakill! Make love to me, baby! I always wanted you to be my first. It feels soooooo good," Laneisha screamed and moaned.

She has the sexiest "fuck faces" that I have ever seen, I thought when she looked at me and bit her lip.

Right then, I felt her walls tighten as her right leg

started shaking and her eyes rolled back.

"Jakill! Jakill! Jakill! I'm cumming! You're making me cum! Please don't stop it." She screamed at the top of her lungs.

"I'm cumming too, baby," I moaned then released.

Laneisha didn't even trip about me not pulling out. That must mean that I done my job well then.

I rolled over onto my back and she climbed on top of me. We just laid there soaked in each other's sweat. Laneisha had her head laying on my chest while she slowly grinded her body against mine.

"No matter if you ever change your lifestyle and we become a couple or not, you'll always be my first love," Laneisha said in her sexy voice.

"And you'll always be my Dream Girl," I replied then kissed her on her forehead.

I had to play my part, so I held her a little bit, thinking about how if her brother, Dusty, was out he wouldn't believe I'm laid up with his little sister. I couldn't help but smile at the thought. That's why I'm glad that I don't have a sister.

"Got my mind right and the Chopper held tight/ Nigga, let me know wutz smackin 2night," the ringtone

alerted me that I had a call.

"Wat's up, D?" I answered after I looked at the Caller ID.

"Cuz, I got the Telly set up like a mufucka. I'm on the way to pick up the actresses right now," D-Slug said and started lighting.

Laneisha began slowly rubbing my chest.

"Yeah though, nigga, I'm definitely there next go round or it's on, cuz. But listen, I'm bout to smack the crib and call it a night."

"Who?" D asked knowing that calling it a night probably meant that I had just beat some pussy up.

"Neisha Boo, can you get me something to drink?" I asked her just to let D-Slug know who I was laid up with without making it obvious.

As soon as she asked me what did I want to drink? D-Slug went crazy on the phone.

"Cuz, you finally hit that? Nigga, I know it was fire. What's it hittin for?" D badgered me.

"Holla at me after ya movie, "I said and ended the call knowing that D was probably mad that he didn't get to Laneisha first.

I managed to escape Laneisha without the extra

talking. I headed home for the night. I was driving on auto pilot as usual because my mind was only thinking about if there was quick lick, we could hit tomorrow so I could get this car money together. Fuck it, we might as well get Spade's bitch ass sooner then I planned, I decided. I safely made it home and was out before my head hit the pillow.

CHAPTER 6

I woke up around 9:00 a.m. and called D-Slug.

"Nigga, you know what time it is?" D complained about me waking him up.

"Yeah, it's time to get money, nigga. Get ya ass up and meet me at the cut crib in an hour."

I heard Tiffs voice in the background.

"Make that two hours, cuz," D-slug replied.

"Aight. but don't bullshit. It's time to play Spades, nigga," I said then hung up thinking about Tiff and Shalynda.

I started picking out one of my 'all purpose' black outfits and decided to call Kia before I hopped in the shower. I know that she has class at 9:30 a.m. so I won't have to talk too long.

She answered on the first ring like she was waiting for me to call. "Hey baby."

"How's the future Mrs. Freeman doin?" I asked her.

"Good now that you called me. You always know how to make me feel good. I miss you, baby, but I'm getting ready to go to class."

Perfect.

"I just wanted to let you know how much you stay on my mind. I'm a let you go to class, baby. I love you, Kia."

"I love you too, JD," Kia said as we ended our quick conversation.

After I took a shower and got dressed in black Dickie's pants and a black T-shirt, I drove around the corner to the cut crib. Big Hurt was the only nigga there at the time. While he was still on the porch I crept down to the basement and grabbed up a Chopper and a drum out of the stashspot. I spent a little bit of time loading it up. Just as I finished, Hurt walked in. We ended up playing Madden on the small TV until D-Slug finally showed up.

"What's the game plan, my nigga?" D-Slug asked me as soon as he walked into the spot.

I got straight to the point. "You know the nigga, Spade, always come ridin through tryin to stunt every day around twelve, trying to get on some young bitches leavin school at lunch," I replied.

Westinghouse High School is The Burgh's Eastside High from *Lean On Me*. You can leave at any time you want to, but lunch time is when all the young freaks leave to go on fuck missions.

I continued, "That means we got about forty-five minutes before he come out his crib. We gonna leave Daz's mom's car here and take Butch's. We gonna park a block away and play the cuts to his crib and wait on him to walk out. Ain't nobody gonna be out on that dry ass block this time of day, so we good. As soon as that door open, we rushin him back in and goin after the work and cheddar. Look under the couch, I got something for you, cuz."

"What, you the hood Santa Claus or something now," D joked as he reached under the couch with Big Hurt's eyes following him to see what I stashed there.

Once D-slug pulled out the chopper with the drum he acted like it was Christmas. He jumped up and down and did some kind of Army pose like he was ducked down in the trenches.

"Oh shit, cuz. I was tweakin for one of these mufuckas, JD. And it got a fuckin drum. Who you cop this off?" He asked.

"You know Lil Erny can get whatever. And he showed love like hell on the price. You know how he be with the family protection comes first. He protected his family right cause he slung me three of em," I responded then continued, "Let's bounce before we miss the bus. I already got mine in the ride."

Hurt had a look on his face like he wanted to ask if he could come on the lick with us, but he already knew the answer to that question. Plus, he knew that he wouldn't bust a gun if he had to.

Me and D-Slug hopped in the car and drove to the end of Rosedale Street, 4 houses away from Spade's house, and parked. Like I figured, nobody was out. I made sure that I kept a good watch on Spade's red brick crib while I got the remaining half of bottle of 151 from under my seat. I took 3 big gulps of it then handed it to D-Slug. He's not really a drinker but he took a couple sips to get his blood pumping. I'm mad as fuck that I forgot to put my Lyfe CD in the car. Fuck it!

"Let's go, cuz." I said.

We quickly put on our masks and crept through a cut that led behind the house that we parked in front of. We had to climb over 3 small fences and one tall wooden fence to get to the back of Spade's crib. Those were no obstacles but the Red Nose Pit Bull that we had to outrun in the 2nd yard gave us a small hurdle that we overcame.

We made our way to the side of Spade's crib and ducked off in the bushes that must not have been trimmed for the whole summer.

"We can chill here till he comes out and then... Before I could finish the sentence, Spade's front door opened.

D seen the door open too, and without saying a word, we both ran out of the cut with choppers aimed at chest level.

Spade was busy looking back in his crib, yelling at somebody inside to hurry up. I can't believe that this nigga dumped on me and is slippin this bad. It's crazy how quickly niggas forget about the constant danger of the game.

When Spade turned back around, all he saw was 2 Choppers at his chest, held by 2 niggas in all black, masks, and gloves. I immediately took the 45 from his hip.

"Get ya bitch ass back in the crib! Who else in there?" D-Slug asked, ready to kill anything moving.

We began backing Spade back into his crib.

"Nobody, I swear, cuz. Homies. Just take my scrilla and leave. Please don't kill me!" Spade begged.

While Spade was copping pleas to D, I was already in one of the bedrooms. I quickly found a little boy hiding under his bed. When I pulled him from under the bed, I immediately knew that he was Spade's son because he looked like a spitting image of Spade. *This will work even better now,* I thought.

"Bring that nigga back here. I found his 'nobody'." I said while holding the little nigga by his collar.

Spade's son still didn't make a sound, but Spade on the other hand began crying like a bitch.

"Please don't kill my son! Leave him out of this! He's only five, man! He ain't got nothing to do with this street shit! Please, I'll give you whatever you want! Just let him go!" Spade pleaded.

I gripped his son's collar tighter. "Take us to the fuckin safe then, or this lil nigga's gonna have a breeze going through him." I said and gave Spade a "Dare Me" look.

"Aright! Aright! It's in the back room."

"Keep ya burner on lil cuz. If this nigga tries some slick shit, kill his son, cuz!" I said to D-Slug as Spade guided us to the master bedroom.

The first thing I noticed in this bedroom was the

huge flat screen TV on the wall and the gigantic circle bed sitting up on some type of platform. That's when I knew for sure that S gave me and D-Slug the blueprint for something beautiful.

"Open it," I calmly said with my Chopper resting on the back of Spade's head.

When Spade finally finished the combination and got ready to open it, I pulled him out of the closet by his long plaits.

"Lay ya punk ass on the floor, nigga." I demanded and made Spade lay face first in the carpet.

D-Slug then made Spade's son lay on the floor next to him. His son still didn't speak a word or do any crying. Spade was still bitching, but I wasn't listening. I was too focused on the safe.

I grabbed a black silk pillowcase off one of the big pillows and went back into the closet. As soon as I opened the safe there was a small 32 revolver staring dead at me. *He must have seen this day comin,* I thought.

I looked out of the closet at Spade, who was still stretched out on the floor next to his son.

"You thought that Triple Crown book shit was gonna work or something?" I jokingly asked, referring to the book publishing company that publishes all "Urban" books that every nigga locked up read a million times.

D-Slug didn't know what the fuck I was talking about until I showed him the little ass gun, then we both started laughing.

"That's definitely only workin in them books, cuz," D said while looking at Spade and shaking his head.

I looked back into the safe and couldn't believe what was looking back at me.

"We hit the fuckin Power Ball, nigga," I said excitedly.

I began taking the money and drugs out of the safe and loading it into the pillowcase. When I was done, I walked out of the closet with my swag turned all the way on. D-Slug just looked at the bag and smiled.

Now that we had what we came for, well, half of what we came for, it was time to finish our mission and get the fuck out of the crime scene.

"D snatch out one of those extension cords and tie up the lil nigga."

"I got it. What we gonna do with pops though?" D-Slug asked like he didn't already know.

"I got something for him," I said as Spade lifted his

head up to try to peek and see what's going on.

D-Slug tied up Spade's son in record time. That boy was tied at his wrist and ankles but was standing straight up like a soldier at attention, and still didn't speak a word. I would have expected him to be crying for his mother or some little kid shit like that, but he was more gangsta than his bitch ass dad.

As soon as Spade lifted his head up, I put my size 12 Jordan's right into his face a couple of times. He began crying again, so D-Slug put one of his Air Max's into Spade's ribs.

"Quit cryin like a bitch, gangsta," D-Slug antagonized him.

"What, you thought that you were gonna clap at me and it just be gravy like I'm a washed-up young nigga or something?" I asked rhetorically.

Spade looked at his son, then back to me.

"I knew it was you behind that mask, JD. Nigga, I'm a kill you JD!" Spade screamed at the top of his lungs.

A devilish grin formed on my face. "How you gonna do that sittin next to Satan?" Those were the last words that he heard before the Chopper took off most of his head, turning his brains into potted meat, and separated his left arm from his body.

That was the first time that I saw exactly what a Chopper was capable of doing, but it was nowhere near the last time.

"Yeah, nigga," D said, excited by the action. "But what about his son? Ol boy said ya handle."

I had thought about that too. The way that Spade looked at his son and then made sure he repeated my name was clearly a way to instruct his son to tell the police that "JD killed my daddy."

I put the Chopper to the boy's head and said to him, "If you tell anybody anything I'll come back and kill you and whoever ya mommy is. You dig me?"

The little nigga just gave me a cold stare and still didn't say a word.

Me and D ran out of the back door straight to the get-away car. We sped to the cut crib with the radio off since we both were half expecting to hear sirens by now. Luckily, gunshots are so common in Homiwood that no sirens were heard until after we parked in the back-alley way cut and was walking into the crib.

I walked in expecting there to be the niggas in there trying to eye-hustle what we had in the bag, but to my surprise the crib was empty. D-Slug ran down in the basement and put his Chopper in the stashspot. When he walked back up the steps, he sat down at the dining room table, where I was at with the bag, and gave me a "You know you fucked up" look.

"Cuz, you know you should have slumped Spade's son after he heard ya name," D-Slug said coldly.

"No old mufuckas or kids unless it's a must," I said even though I had the feeling that the decision to not kill the little nigga would come back to haunt me someway somehow. "And how many nigga's names are initials, D-Slug? He'll probably fuck up the initials before the pigs even get there," I said more to convince myself than D-Slug.

D-Slug brushed that situation off and grabbed the pillowcase that was sitting in the middle of the table. "Fuck it. What's in this mufucka though? Fuck the suspense and shit," he said and poured the contents onto the table.

It was like the table was glowing.

"Yeah, nigga, we straight," D-Slug said excitedly as he grabbed a handful of money.

"Cuz, we're nowhere near straight. We need at least

two more licks like this before we can stop jackin mufuckas," I responded.

We sat there and counted what we thought would be around $100,000. It ended up only amounting to $46,000. But we also now had 3 birds (kilos) of coke.

I gave D-Slug $15,000 and I kept the same amount.

D looked at the remaining $15,000 still sitting in a pile on the table. "What we doin with the rest?"

"We putting that up in a stash at my mom's crib. D, we both know we bout to blow most of our scrill on all types of shit. Oh yeah, I forgot to tell you Butch is taking me to go cop a ride in the morning," I slipped that sentence in and then continued, "The fifteen stacks are gonna start our lawyer fee and emergency stash. We got to have money put up for a rainy day cause you know how much it rains in the hood. Dig me?" I asked to make sure that we were on the same page.

"Yeah, I'm with you. I dig that," D replied while fanning his face with money. "What about the work though?"

I grabbed a stack of bills and began to fan myself too. "As far as birds, we can't just come out of the blue with a lot of work, or niggas is gonna add and get four.

What we got to do is cook this shit up and slang half and quarter zips to all the block niggas." I said and remembered that neither me or D-Slug knew how to cook up crack. "We'll look like regular niggas that probably only got four and a half on the stove.

We already gonna be usual suspects anyway, but as long as we don't do no extra shit, it will just be rumors."

D started fanning his face with 2 stacks of money now. "What about that car you coppin?" he said, letting me know that he heard everything that I had said. "And I know you got more on ya mind."

"I'm copping a regular hood ride just to get around in and I want to get a lil apartment out by I.U.P. since it's in the cut," I said and picked up another stack to fan myself with following D-Slug's stuntin lead.

"And it's where Kia's at." D laughed then continued, "Damn nigga. She gives you the pussy, now you buyin her cribs and shit."

D-Slug laughed until a tear dropped.

I admit, it was funny, and I laughed too, knowing that Kia got me fucked up in the head a little bit.

"You should get you a spot in the cut and a lil ride too though cause it's about to get heavy for us and niggas might end up on our heels one day. Cuz, if you get a spot though, don't take just any lil smut there, cause they be the ones that set ya ass up." I said to D with all seriousness.

Even though I'm only a year older than D-Slug, I been through a lot more and S always kept my mind booted up above niggas my age. So, D never takes it as I'm trying to make him feel like my young nigga. He knows that I plan and think shit out way before he does. So, I put him on game so that he don't find himself in a bad situation.

"Yo, I'm bout to hit the mall. Is you rollin?" D-slug asked as he got up from the table and stuffed money into all of his pockets.

"That shit's bumin. holes in ya pockets already, huh," I laughed and continued, "Naw though. I'm bout to fly S some more Cheddar and go show my face around the Ave."

"Yeah, you just reminded me, nigga. What went down with you and Virgin Mary?" D asked, referring to Laneisha.

I knew that I had a stripe that he wanted so I took the time to stunt on him. "Cuz, you know how you get the smut movie shit, right, well, I get the Box Office Oscar

Award winning shit. You know me, and she respect game. Talking bout she always wanted me to be her first and shit, nigga. They always want you to be their hundredth," I joked and stunted.

 We laughed for a minute.

 Before we left the crib, I put the work in the stashspot with the 2 Choppers. I then grabbed my Chopper and me and D walked out of the back door. I looked at the clock on my cell phone and noticed that we were in the crib bullshitting for about 3 hours.

 "Yo, I'm a get somebody to cook that shit up probably the day after tomorrow. We ain't in no rush. Niggas know better than to go in the stash, if they even figured out where our stash is. I don't give a fuck if they from The Tre. All they got to do is wait, and they'll be gravy when we're straight," I said as I pounded up D-Slug.

 "I'm a hit you up when I get back from the mall, cuz," D said and started walking through the side cut to the front of the house.

 "Oh yeah, have that tape with you too when you come back, and find out when the next party's gonna be," I hollered and walked to the fiend buggie.

CHAPTER 7

I got to my mom's crib and went straight to my room. After recounting my money and the lawyer fee again just to do it, I put the lawyer fee inside of the wall in my room. It was a hole the size of a softball in the plaster wall that my foot made during one of me and D-Slug's wrestling matches. The hole was just big enough for me to stick my hand into and sit the money on a long ledge that was inside of the wall for no reason.

I then took $8,000 from my $15,500 and put it in between my mattress. I had to make sure I hold on to that to pay for the apartment I was planning on getting and to put some furniture in it. I got a pint of vodka out of my bottom drawer and took a few gulps while trying to figure out what music I want to listen to.

"Go my mind right and the Chopper held tight/ Nigga let me know wutz smackin 2night/'

"What's up, baby." I answered the ringtone.

"Hey, baby. What you been doing all day?" Kia asked.

"Just chillin with D for a minute."

"I miss you."

See, that's what I love about Kia. Any other woman would have been asking if any bitches was with us, because everybody knows that D-Slug always has a hook-up lined up. But Kia trust me like crazy. *I don't know why though.*

I took a sip of vodka. I got to cut my freak bitches off. but I'm still gonna knock off Laneisha some more, but she doesn't count, I thought. It sounds good.

"Yeah, baby, I got something special planned for you this weekend. Instead of you goin home, we gonna stay up there. Is that cool?" I asked.

"Yes, baby. My roommate is going home for the weekend, so we'll be all alone."

I took 2 big gulps while thinking about what happened when Kia's roommate was gone the other day. "I'm a drive-up Friday afternoon, "I said.

I finally decided on turning on Master P's Ghetto Dope CD. I could have been fly and put on some slow songs while Kia was on the phone, but the liquor was starting to boost up the buzz that I already had, and I needed some gangsta shit on. I don't know why I turned on the song "Captain Kirk" though.

We talked until almost 6 p.m. After all the lovey dovey shit that a nigga got to say to his woman was said, we hung up. That's when it hit me that *I had forgot to send S that money before Quik-Cash closed. I'm sure that he didn't run through a stack in 2 days though,* I thought.

I took 2 more sips from the bottle and then put it back in the drawer next to the box of baggies. Then I put $7,500 in my pockets, made sure that I turned off the sounds, since my mom always be complaining about me leaving them on, and then I was headed out of the door to Butch's car.

I pulled up in the small low-key parking lot behind the row housed on the Ave. and hopped out. There were 2 smokers sitting on the broken glass covered cement steps, looking like I fucked up what they were about to do. Once they saw that it was me, they began unrolling their washcloths that held their works.

Just my luck, the fiends weren't the only people chillin in the back. I looked up and saw Keva standing on the backfire escape, smoking on a green leaf. The way these row houses were built, every 4 cribs had their own fire escape. The fire escapes weren't the kind that come down the side of the spot, they were indented into the building so that they created a small walkway that led to the basements and created nice cuts. The only thing that I found crazy was the fact that the fire escape was made out of wood.

Keva looked down from the second landing. "What's up, JD? Can a bitch get some company till I'm done smoking?" she asked.

I finally caught her alone, I thought. I casually walked up the wooden steps, trying not to make my eagerness too noticeable.

"What's smackin? Why you out here with only a long ass T-shirt on?" I asked while looking at her sexy legs, remembering just how good her pussy was.

"I ain't got nothing to hide, nigga. It's only you up here with me."

"Oh, 'only you,' huh? How I go from 'Daddy' to 'only you'?" I asked with a devilish grin and a motive.

She took a long, extended hit of her weed and then threw the roach. The way she sucked on that blunt made me mad at myself for never getting any head from her.

"You know you'll always, always, always be my daddy. Drizzy just be blockin all the fuckin time," Keva replied.

"Where that nigga at anyway?"

"Who knows where that broke ass nigga's at. I want to know where my big soldier's at? Is he standing at attention for me?"

She had to know that I was hard as a brick, so I didn't respond. I just looked down at my shorts, then back up at her.

Keva seductively licked her lips and asked, "Can I get some of that good dick before Drizzy get back?"

"Oh, you missed this dick, Keva," I teased and grabbed my dick through my shorts for emphasis.

"You already know. 1 need that dick. Daddy."

I never been one to turn down somebody in need.

Keva turned around slowly showing me her ass, which was sitting out from under the T-shirt. She backed her ass up into me and grinded it on my dick. Then she pulled her shirt up around her waist and pulled my dick out of my shorts.

"Damn I miss this dick," Keva softly said as she slowly stroked it a few times.

I leaned my head back and decided to just let her do what she do.

Keva bent over, pulled her pink thong to the side, and slowly rubbed my dick up and down her ass crack. I began tweaking even more than ever. *This is what I been trying to get back for a while now and it's right here*, I thought.

As soon as Keva finally put the tip of my dick inside of her dripping wet pussy, all I heard was, *"Got my mind right and the Chopper held tight/ Nigga let me know wutz smackin 2 night."*

I answered my cell phone as quickly as possible, intending on telling whoever to call me back. I should have let my phone go to Voice Mail, but I guess a higher power felt that I was about to do some dumb shit by fucking her and forced me to answer the phone. "Yo?"

"What's up, Jakill? I see your rental out back. Where you at cause I want to see you?" Laneisha asked.

I immediately sobered up a little bit and my dick got a little soft as I pulled the head out of Keva. I motioned with my finger for Keva to be quiet. I knew that she wouldn't say a word because she got more at risk than me.

"I'm at the park. Give me five minutes. Aight, sexy?" I had to make it sound good to her.

I hung up and looked at Keva, who was standing

there playing with herself and licking her lips at me. She walked back over to me and reached for my dick, but I put it back in my pants before she could grab it. That might have been the hardest thing I ever had to do in my life. I was literally going to war with my dick because it was trying its hardest to jump out of my shorts.

"What's wrong? Who was that?" Keva asked, assuming that something bad had to have happened to make me put my dick away.

"Listen we both almost fucked up. Yeah, I always be thinkin bout still fuckin you, and you got the best pussy I ever had, but Drizzy love you to death, and me and Laneisha is cool as fuck," I said.

Keva looked at me with a puzzled expression. "So that was Laneisha? Oh, you got that virgin pussy," she said as if she was cool with the situation. "I feel you. I just can't believe I let you slip away. You supposed to be here with us, not Drizzy. It's cool though. Don't worry, I ain't gonna say shit. You know I can keep a secret. Plus, I'll always have love for you cause you my nigga regardless.

My dick was completely soft by now.

"That's real shit, but if we ever be under different circumstances, it's me and you again. No doubt. Let me ya bathroom real quick though."

Keva guided me into her mom's crib to the bathroom. She stood at the door for a second, clearly debating on coming in the bathroom with me and trying to fuck again.

I guess she ruled against it, because she walked away. I quickly closed and locked the door because I started tweaking again. Instead of going after Keva like my dick was telling me to do, I grabbed the closest rag to the sink and washed Keva's juices off me.

Before I ran out of Keva's spot I gave her $100. "Here, take this and get Pooh something. And tell Drizzy I said holla at me if he tryin to get right with some work," I said and left.

Instead of going through the cut straight to Laneisha's front door, I ran around the block so that I could come from the direction of the park. Plus, I had to build up a little bit of perspiration to cover up the soap smell. *I know Laneisha is not my woman, but I'm used to the bullshit from other broads, so I guess it's a habit I have to cover up all tracks of being around other females,* I thought as I jogged down the block.

By now, Laneisha was sitting on her front steps with

Keva's younger sister, Mia. Mia looked like Keva's identical twin, besides in the thickness department. She was a little thin with small titties but had a small bubble ass. Mia was definitely sexy though. Me and her had a thing for each other at one point as well but we never got the chance to fuck. So, we just ended up real cool. That's how I know all about her low-key fuck missions—and there was a lot of them.

"What's up, JD?" Mia asked as I walked up and she was getting up to leave.

"Ain't shit smackin but the usual."

Mia walked away switching her bubble. It took everything inside of me not to follow her ass with my eyes. So, I stole a quick glance and then turned all of my attention to Laneisha.

"What's smackin, Neisha Boo? What was you bored or something," I joked.

She sucked her teeth. "No. I just wanted to see you. You know you always stop pass this time of day," Laneisa replied.

"I was postin up with D-Slug for a lil bit," I lied for no reason.

"Why D don't come up here as much as he used to?"

she asked curiously.

"You know cuz always be chickenhead Chasin." I said and we both laughed at the truth.

"Maybe we should hook up him and Mia," Laneisha suggested.

"They definitely right for each other." I said wondering if she caught on to my ignorant inside joke.

Laneisha stood up and began slowly walking up her steps. "Do you want to come inside and chill for a little bit?" She asked knowing that I wouldn't refuse.

After 2½ hours of pussy licking, raw dog fucking, and three nuts busted Laneisha was asleep and I was walking out of her back door. I got a big day planned for tomorrow, so I guess I'll hit the crib to get something to sip on and go to sleep for a minute, I thought.

CHAPTER 8

I woke up at 7:30 a.m. and immediately checked my phone as I'm accustomed to do every morning. I went to sleep as soon as I walked in the door last night and I must have been exhausted, I thought as I realized that J-Meanmug didn't wake me up once out of 10 missed calls.

I yawned and checked my voice mail. I had 2 messages from D-Slug talking about some hoes that he had met at the mall, 3 from Kia missing me, and 5 from a couple of young freaks that I stopped calling. I'll call D-Slug and Kia back later, I decided and walked downstairs to the bathroom.

After the longest morning piss that I have ever taken my entire life, I took a shower and got cleaned up. The only thing I was thinking about was what kind of car that I should buy. I even daydreamed for a second about buying a Bently.

I looked in the mirror one more time before I left the bathroom.

Then I went back into my room and began getting as

fly as possible. I put on my royal blue Gucci Vallore sweat suit, all white wifebeater, blue tint Gucci shades, and all white Air Force 1's.

Once I laced up my shoes I walked over to my dresser and opened the top drawer, which held all my jewelry. It's not like I have so much ice that the room lit up or no shit like that, but my neck gets goosebumps just by looking at that drawer.

I topped off my wardrobe with Lil Face's husky Cuban Link with the iced-out cross on it. Then I picked up my new collector's item and put Spade's Jacob on my wrist. *I love jackin*, I thought and laughed.

I looked like a million bucks literally. So, I put on a dab of Egyptian Musk and smelled like a million bucks too.

I put $7,400 in my pockets, which instantly made them bulge. Then I walked out of my mom's crib smiling like I don't have a single care in the world.

When I got into the car, I called Butch. "You woke, Butch?"

"You know damn well I be woken every day at the crack of dawn," Butch replied.

I couldn't determine if that was meant as a crackhead joke or not. "I'll be there in a couple minutes," I said then hung up.

The ride to Butch's crib was only a couple of seconds. Butch was already standing on the curb, rocking back and forth on his heels, when I pulled up. *This smoker can't wait to get his hands on that $300,* I thought.

When he got into the car, he was smiling so hard that I could count all the missing teeth in his mouth.

"I saw this dealership out McMurray Township that be having some hard ass used rides," I said as Butch adjusted his seat for his 6' 3" frame.

"Why don't you just get a new one?"

"I'll give you three letters why I won't," I said and paused long enough to allow him to catch on. "If I come through straight off the lot, I'm getting booked ASAP. Especially when they run the plates and it come back to you," I said and couldn't help but laugh.

"Lil nigga, I used to stay in the sharpest new Caddy and had all the flyest ladies," Butch responded and was getting ready to go into his pre-fiend stories.

All smokers have the same stories. How could have all of them been getting money and all the fiend broads were the baddest bitches in the world? If you ask the next fiend you see about his past I guarantee he say that he was "That Nigga" and had a Caddy. My only problem with that is that if they all were getting money, who were they slangin to? I guess that line is cooked into the crack and they inherit it with that first hit.

Before Butch could relive his past I immediately reached into my bag on the back seat and grabbed the J-Meanmug CD.

J-Meanmug's CDs are all classic shit. I still can't believe that he be making them from Graterford Penitentiary and getting them snuck out. Plus, he makes all of his own beats on a bullshit keyboard that the jail lets niggas buy. On top of that, the nigga is doing this shit while he tries to give back a life sentence on appeal. How real is that?

I put on his Vol. 3 CD and turned on song #3 called *"So Fresh"* featuring the nigga, Dub aka Raw Meat, and let it bang. *"You know I stay so fresh and so clean/ Just finished polishin the AR-J5/ You could tell I'm a gangsta by the way that I lean/ Every niggas nightmare and every hoe's dream."*

We arrived at the dealership in the white man's land and was approached by a white dealer Dave, as soon as we stepped out of the car. Instead of Dave having that stereotypical look on his face like we were there to rob them, he looked like he could already see a car driving off the lot.

Once I explained to Dave that I didn't want to buy the new Lexus that was parked directly in front of us and was only interested in an old school, he walked us up to the top lot that had all of their hard old school muscle cars.

I was only planning on buying a regular hood bucket but once I saw all of those cars those plans when right out of the window.

There were Monte Carlo SS's, Regals, Cutlass's, 5.0s, Grand Nationals, and 4 Iroc Z's in different colors.

What immediately caught my eye was a white with royal blue bowling ball paint job Iroc Z. It was sitting on royal blue painted Iroc rims that had a white stripe painted around them. It had tinted windows and T-Tops.

I opened up the driver door and was speechless. The entire interior was royal blue with white piping, knobs, gear shifter, pedals, and door handles. It even had the professional race car bucket seats. *This motherfucker is matching my outfit*, I thought.

I had always wanted an Iroc Z since the nigga,

Scooter had one that was shitting on all the other cars in the hood back in the day. But this Iroc was shitting on his.

I was already hooked, but to reel me in Dave said, "You gotta see what's in the trunk, buddy."

I followed his lead to the back of the car, expecting to see some regular subs and an amp or some bullshit like that.

Dave opened the trunk slowly. When the trunk lid opened all the way I saw the 2 15" subs built into the back of the back seats with 2 1200wt amps and 2 crossovers attached to the back of the speaker box. What was even more impressive was that all that shit was made by Punch. *I hate when pieces of the sounds be made by all different motherfuckers.* I thought as I noticed that the car even had a spare tire that matched the other tires.

This car even made Butch say, "This mufucker puts all my Caddy's to shame."

All I was thinking about was shitting on all the oldheads and becoming one of The Burgh's flyest niggas.

"How much?" I asked Dave.

"I was looking for around six grand" he replied.

"I got five in cash right now," I bargained.

"Fifty-five."

"Let's sign the papers then," I said and began walking back down the small hill.

It took Butch and Dave about a half hour to complete the paperwork. Then me and Butch walked out front of the building just as Dave's female assistant was pulling up in my new car. She looked good, but my car looked better, so I didn't even think about getting on her.

I counted out $300 as I walked Butch to his car and gave it to him. Then I told him to follow me to the block because I had to holla at him about something. Before I walked back to my car, I grabbed all my CDs out of his car.

When I got into my new head turner, I adjusted the seat and mirrors, then started it up. I revved up the 350 a couple of times and felt like the car was going to flip over the way that the back of it was raising up. Then I put in the B.G. CD *"Life After Cash Money"* and let his song called *"Don't Talk To Me"* turn the trunk into a live concert. I only had the volume on 5 and the bass was banging so hard that I realized that I had adjusted the mirrors for no reason when they vibrated to spots that I didn't set. On top of that, my head felt like it was about to explode.

Butch followed me as I took the longest way

possible back to the block. He started to get out of his car when we pulled up, but I quickly stopped him.

"I thought you had to holla at me," Butch said confused.

"Naw. I just forgot to get something out the trunk. Hit the button for me," I replied and walked to the back of the car.

As soon as he opened the trunk, I wrapped an old towel, that was in the trunk, around the Chopper and put it inside of the trunk of my car. The block was still empty so I'm sure nobody seen the switch.

"What's that?" Butch asked with his head stretching out of the window.

"Mine." I replied, letting him know to mind his business. "I'm a holla at you later, and I'm a send Boo at you. Treat him like he's me. Don't try no funny shit with me."

"You ain't gotta worry bout that, lil nigga."

I gave him $50 more and told him that it was for the gas. He rode off and forgot all about trying to figure out what it was that I had in his trunk.

I got in my new car and drove straight to J & B's Detail Shop to get my car done up. J & B's is a spot on the top of the Ave. where nobody be at, and they wash the cars on the side of the building, so you can be ducked off. I didn't want anybody to know who was sitting behind the tints until my righthand knew first.

While I was waiting for my car to be completed, I called D-Slug. "What's smackin, cuz?" I asked as soon as he answered.

"Is you bout to get ya ride?" D asked.

"Naw, nigga. I already got it. Yo, you know how I said no extra shit, right?"

"Yeah, cuz. What you do?"

I looked at my Iroc Z. "Nigga, fuck that shit. You only live once. Ball out and if niggas catch on, I'll slump whoever. I just copped the hardest Iroc ever! I can't even explain it. I got to show you. Where you at?" I asked excitedly.

"Nigga, you know where I'm at. The Sunrise Inn with a young freak." He replied.

"How you got five stacks in ya pockets and you still fuckin with the dirty ass Sunrise?" I joked.

D-Slug laughed. "You won't believe I ran through four stacks last night on a lot of bullshit at the mall."

"Yeah, I definitely believe it. But look, don't spend

no more change until I pick you up. Drop off ol girl and meet me on the block in a half hour."

"I'll be there. Holla," D-Slug said as we hung up.

I was about to call Kia when B said, "JD, ya shit's done," and tossed me my keys.

My car was shining like a motherfucker and I couldn't wait for niggas to see me hopping out of it. After I admired my car for a second, I gave B $50 and then let the low pros spin out.

I drove up East Hills just to burn some time, but nobody was out. So, I rode the back way through Wilkinsburg. There were a few niggas walking down Penn Ave and a couple broads standing in front of the liquor spot. All eyes were on me. Then I made my way back to the block.

I pulled up in front of the cut crib and couldn't believe that D-Slug went and gathered all the block niggas with him. Everybody was standing in front of the spot waiting on me to pull up. They all probably expected me to pull up in a regular Regal or something like that. That's probably why they didn't even think that it was me behind the tinted windows of the car. They stared as I was driving towards them.

As soon as the tinted windows went down niggas started going fucking crazy.

"Yo, that shit is sick, cuz." E-Wok said.

"Cuz, you got to put me on with y'all niggas cause I need one of those." Teeke said.

"That's what the fuck I'm talkin bout, JD. You killin em." Boo said with his approval.

D-Slug was just looking at every inch of my car speechless.

"D, you like it?" I asked.

"Nigga, do I like it? I love this shit! What it run you?" D asked but quickly continued, knowing that I wouldn't talk numbers in front of other niggas, "Yeah, you got to get ol boy to take me to cop something tomorrow, cuz. Fuck that."

"I got you," I said then looked at the rest of the niggas. "All the rest of y'all just give us a second and y'all will be right too, homies." I said honestly. "D, help me take off the tops and put them in the spot."

We put the glass in the crib while the other niggas examined my car. *One of these niggas is probably thinking about jacking me right now.* I thought as me and D-Slug were walking back out of the house and I saw niggas facial expressions.

Before I could even tell D-Slug to hop in, he was already in the car going through the CDs and telling the other niggas that we'll holla at them later.

"We'll be back in a minute." I said as I got into my car and peeled off some of the back tires.

"Cuz, put this old Big Tymers CD on. All those Mannie Fresh beats is the shit." D suggested.

He's right. I thought. Plus, they got the perfect song for me right now. I put on the song called *"#1 Stunna"* and the sounds went fucking crazy like the speakers are about to jump out of the box.

D-Slug leaned his seat all the way back and began rolling up some dro.

We rode around for a minute, then pulled up in front of Butch's crib. *He was standing there with a gang of smokers with him. I guess he looked out for all of them with that $300.* I thought. Butch walked up to the car when I turned the sounds down low.

"I see you got it shined up already, lil nigga," Butch said.

I took my shades from the back seat and put them on. "Yea, I got to shine, Butch. Look though, I want to go back out there tomorrow and get D a car."

Instead of speaking, D-Slug lit up his blunt, which had his mind's full attention at the time.

"Same price? What time?" Butch asked.

"Same price. Same time." I said and pulled off while he was still leaning on the car door.

CHAPTER 9

I had almost forgot again to send S some more money. We drove to the Quik-Cash across the street from One Stop Store on Brushton Ave. D gave me $500 to send to S, so I matched him and got a money order for a stack. I put it in an envelope and sent it off right then and there.

When I walked back out of Quik-Cash D was leaning out of the car trying to get some young broad to walk across the street to him. She was acting like he wasn't shit because he was in the passenger seat. When she saw me, she locked her eyes on me and gave me that look. I meanmugged her and hopped in the car.

"It's two o'clock and you know Keva's sister, Mia, is probably gonna be with Laneisha." I hinted to D-Slug as we pulled off.

D sat up in his seat. "I heard she got the best head in the hood, cuz. I definitely wouldn't mind judging that talent show." He said and looked up in the sky like he could actually see it.

"They let out in fifteen minutes. That give me a lil

bit to holla at Kia."

I hate talking to a woman while one of the niggas is around, because they will have all the jokes in the world—especially D-Slug.

"What's up, baby girl? Was you thinkin bout me?" I asked into the phone.

"You already know, baby. How come you didn't call me back last night? I wanted to hear ya voice before I went to sleep." Kia said in her fake sad tone.

D-Slug was leaned back rolling up another blunt and acting like he wasn't ear hustling my conversation with Kia.

I turned the sounds on real low. "I had to get up early so I could go buy my car. So, I had to go to sleep early." I responded to Kia.

"What kind did you get?"

"A hard ass Iroc Z. I'm a show you in a couple days, and I still got a surprise for you." I replied wondering if she knew what an Iroc Z was.

"I love you, Kia." D-Slug screamed into my earpiece jokingly.

"That boy is crazy. He didn't buy a car too?" Kia asked.

"Nope. I'm taking him to get one tomorrow though." I said thinking about how I'm going to have to buy Kia a car when we get our spot out there.

I spent the next few minutes talking to her until me and D got 2 blocks away from Westinghouse. Then I lied to Kia and told her that I had to call her back because "me and D bout to walk into the mall right now."

We pulled up on the side of the school just as everybody began running out of the school. *I can't believe that I'm sitting in this hard ass Iroc and there are niggas my age running out of that door flat broke thinking that an education is going to get them some money.* I thought.

"Bingo." D-Slug said, pointing in the direction of where Laneisha and Mia were standing on the corner talking to their friends.

I hurried up and put on Tyrese's old CD and turned on *"Sweet Lady"*. Then I turned the sounds up to 6. (Yeah, I'm simpin, so what!)

Everybody's heads turned in our direction immediately. We slowly pulled up on Laneisha and Mia. I drove slowly that damn near half of the song had played by the time that I had got directly on the side of them.

Laneisha was all smiles when she saw that it was me

behind the wheel. It was like a movie being played in slow motion because I couldn't hear shit and all I saw was motherfuckers staring and pointing and saying shit that I could not hear. I knew right then and there that I made at least one nigga decide to drop out of school and get some real money.

I hit the mute button, which actually just cuts off the highs and turns down the lows so that you can still feel the bass vibrating the car.

Laneisha slowly and seductively walked to the driver's door with Mia in tow.

"You know you too sexy to be walkin, baby." I said to Laneisha.

"Is that right, Jakill?" She responded.

"No doubt. Neisha Boo."

"Whose car is this?" Mia asked curiously.

"Who's drivin it? I just copped it this morning." I nodded my head at a group of young niggas that I knew. Then I looked back at Laneisha, who was now leaning on my car with one hand and had her other hand on her hip like she was modeling my car. "Is yall hoppin in though or is we gonna talk over them loud ass horns behind us?" I asked.

They hopped in the back seat and I turned the sounds up to 3. That shit was still banging like fuck. There was no need for us to do any talking at the time anyway because we were all feeling the life at that moment. I just kept looking into the rearview mirror because Laneisha would seductively lick her lips at me every time. That was all the communication that I needed.

We pulled up at my mom's crib and I left the sounds on as I got out and had them wait in the car. When I got out of the car my mom was just coming out of the front door. She looked at me. then the car, then back at me and just shook her head. I ran right past her without saying a word.

I ran up into my room and grabbed $2,000 from under my mattress. *There go the flat screen TV*. I thought. I was running back out of the crib 30 seconds after I went in.

I got back in my car just as Tyrese's song, *"Lately"*, was coming on. I checked the traffic and then pulled off.

Nobody asked where we were going or anything. They just enjoyed the ride. We rode around the hood for a minute and then through East Liberty to just shit on whoever was posted up by David's Shoes. Then we drove out to Monroeville Mall. I had already decided to buy Laneisha some shit just to add to this stuntastic day.

Once we found a close parking spot we hopped out. I don't know about anybody else, but my legs were still vibrating. Mia was the last one getting out of the car and she had the nerve to lock the doors.

"Good lookin, Mia, but if somebody's trying to get in my ride, they don't have to open the door since half of my roof is off." I said, and we all started laughing.

That made me think though. *Next time I got to keep the tops in the trunk with the Chopper.*

We walked into the already crowded mall. *I don't give a fuck who I run in to just as long as it ain't Kia*, I thought. For some reason it felt like it was more women at the mall today than any other day just because I have a woman with me. That's when I noticed that me and Laneisha was pretty much matching each other's outfits.

I had on the royal blue sweatsuit hook up, and Laneisha had on blue Baby Phat jeans, a white and royal blue Baby Phat belly-shirt, and all white Air Force 1's.

The entire mall was looking at us like we were the couple of the year or some shit.

Being that I planned on spending some change on

Laneisha I decided that it would be better if me and her split up from D-Slug and Mia so that I don't put any pressure on him.

"We'll meet back up with y'all at the food court in two hours." I said once we passed Foot Locker.

Here I am about to out trick the "Trick Master." I thought and laughed to myself.

I expected to be in the first women's store that we walked into for at least an hour while Laneisha looked around like most women do, but she only looked at a few things. The item that she really wanted was a regular black coach belt. But what really surprised me was when she walked to the register and paid for it herself without her even thinking about asking me to pay for it.

Laneisha's job at Old Navy is holding her down. I thought as we walked out of the first store.

Little did Laneisha know that she had just passed a test that majority of women fail. Most broads would have gone to the most expensive thing in the store and then put their hand out. So, I walked her into the next store that had a lot of Coogi shit. I had seen a red and multi-colored Coogi dress the last time that me and D was out here chillin and I know that it would look perfect on her.

We walked around the store, and I acted like I already didn't have my eyes locked on that dress hanging up on the wall. When we walked by it, I asked her if she liked it.

Laneisha looked at the price tag. "I like it, but I definitely can't afford it." She replied and began to walk away to look at something else.

She stopped when she heard me call over the salesperson to get the dress.

I pulled out a stack of money. "You definitely can afford it Neisha Boo," I said as I led her to the counter.

"You don't have to buy that for me, Jakill."

"I know I don't have to, but that's why I want to. Feel me?"

She just stood there with a look of amazement on her face.

Every other minute she gives me a reason why she should be my woman, but I still know that she wouldn't be anywhere near the rider that Kia would be. I thought as we walked into the women's shoe store.

I put a nice dent into my money by the time that I bought Laneisha a pair of stilettos, a pair of Lady's Air Maxs, and a small Figuro chain with a small heart on it.

We had one more stop to make before this tricking adventure was over. We walked into Victoria's Secret. Within 5 minutes I had picked out this sexy ass red laced get-up for her. Something about red laced shit makes me go crazy.

"Is this what you want to see me in tonight, Jakill?" Laneisha asked teasingly.

I gave her a devilish grin. "At first."

She blushed. "Baby, you always know how to make me feel special." She said and kissed me on my cheek.

Knowing where this conversation could go, I changed it. "We were supposed to meet D and Mia like fifteen minutes ago." I said while looking at my Jacob.

D-Slug and Mia were already sitting down eating when we walked up to the table. I immediately noticed the 6-8 bags sitting next to Mia on the floor, but I didn't comment on them.

Me and Laneisha helped them knock the rest of the pizza and then we all headed out to the car. Laneisha and Mia walked in front of us, talking about what me and D bought them.

I slowed down me and D's pace so that we were out of hearing range. "Cuz, Mia got like six bags. I know you ain't blow that much on her?" I asked D-Slug seriously.

He looked at me and laughed like the mad scientist. "Nigga, I would of, got her twenty bags. I took her in Raves cheap ass store and let her tear it down. I only blew three hunnit and some change in there. Plus, I copped her those S. Carter shoes. If the head's good as niggas say, it's worth it. You know they say, 'it ain't trickin if you got it." D-Slug said and convinced me that he had a good strategy.

I was trying to keep my laugh low as I thought about the cheap shit Mia probably had in her bag. "I can't believe she let you take her in Raves." I said and laughed again. "Shit, I just spent more than that on one fuckin dress for Laneisha."

"Yeah, but y'all got somethin." He responded, and I nodded in agreement.

When we got into my car, I immediately checked to make sure all my shit, was still in it. I'm never leaving my tops again, I thought.

I put on that old Silk CD and let *"Meeting In My Bedroom"* set the mood as we slowly pulled off. While Laneisha and Mia sang along, me and D were both zoned out. I don't know what he was thinking about, but I'm debating on who our next lick is going to be.

Either Jeff Rose or Tim Murphy. Those 2 niggas are eating. You know a nigga is getting major money if he goes by his full government name. Jeff is one of the Cora Street niggas. He been getting money for a minute and washing it through his corner store so that he doesn't be too hot. The nigga even had a new Benz that he never drove but kept parked on Cora St. 24/7 just to say that he is That Nigga from Cora St., I guess.

As far as Tim, he's an old school type of nigga that been getting it since he used to post up in the hood, Point Breeze, in the late 80's. He's a trickin ass nigga. I mean the type that will tell a broad off top that he got $500 for some pussy. His money is long as fuck, so it really didn't matter to him.

All I know is that we got to get them perfectly though because they can put change on our heads, and it won't even compare to their trick bills for the month. I'm killing both of them then so that they can't even figure out who got them, I decided.

I must have been on auto pilot as usual, because I wasn't even paying any attention to driving, but I got us to the Holiday Inn safely. Since we were all underage, me and D-Slug had to give the motherfucker an extra $100 a piece to put in his pockets for 2 rooms.

D-Slug grabbed Mia's hand as soon as he got his room key. "I'll holla at you at eight so, we can go get my ride." D said and gave me a pound before they damn near ran to the elevator.

"Nigga, you better have her gone off you in the morning." I hollered to him.

I grabbed Laneisha's hand and guided her to the other elevator. When we got on the elevator, she faced me, and we began kissing until the door opened on the next floor and an old white lady got on. For the rest of the ride we just stared into each other's lust filled eyes and waited to hear the elevator make that "ding" sound on our floor.

Ding!

As soon as we walked into our room and the door closed, we started going at it, kissing and shit. I told her to go into the bathroom and get the shower running and I would be right behind her in a second. When she turned her back to walk away, I quickly took the SIM card out of my phone and put it in between the pages of the Bible that was sitting on top of the dresser. I had my phone off all day, but she might be a low key nosey one.

I walked into the large bathroom and looked at

Laneisha standing in the shower with water running down her curvaceous frame. I couldn't help but realize exactly how sexy she is.

Laneisha put both of her hands on her hips and looked at me. "Are you going to get in with me or are you going to take a picture?" She sarcastically asked and smiled.

That wouldn't be a bad idea. I thought.

She gave me a "hell no" look like she had read my thought.

"I'm just admiring how sexy you are." I said in my "Quiet Storm" voice.

She slowly licked her lips. "Let me see something too then," she said then seductively looked me up and down.

I took off my clothes a little quicker than I should have because I had to have looked like I was tweaking—which I was—and also because I almost tripped when I tried to get out of both pants legs at the same time by doing what looked like the Running Man dance. I caught my balance though and was back in action even though Laneisha giggled at me for almost falling.

I got in the shower with my dick harder than it has

ever been, but I had to play it cool. I lathered up a rag and began slowly washing Laneisha's entire body. She softly moaned as I used the rag to caress her most sensitive spots. She then returned the wash and took her time as well. When she washed my dick in slow motion, I almost busted out, but I held back long enough for her to move on to a different body part.

After about 45 minutes of teasing each other, we dried each other off and went back into the bedroom. I started passionately kissing her until she pulled back and stopped me.

"Wait. I got something for you." Lakeisha said while going into the Vicky bag that she brought into the room with her.

I laid back on the bed while she put on the red laced get-up and modeled for me. That little shit fit her perfect and I swear she looked like America's Next Top Model.

I gave her a smile of approval.

Then she began dancing a little bit for me. She was doing some Jamaican "wind" dances. Whatever song that she had in her head was the exact same song in mine because I was subconsciously nodding my head to the unheard music like her body was hypnotizing me. I was holding my dick in my hands while I watched.

Once I couldn't take it anymore, I pulled her to me by her waist and laid her on the bed. She immediately rolled me over on my back and rubbed my chest.

"Baby, as much as you please me, it's time for me to start returning the favor." She said and began kissing down my chest and stomach.

First an Iroc and now this. I thought as I closed my eyes. My eyes opened back up when Laneisha stopped right below my belly button.

Before I could say anything to encourage her to keep going, she looked up at me. "Jakill, you know I never done this before, but I feel like I should. I need you to tell me if I'm doing it right. Aight?" She asked.

She had caught me off guard with that so all I could say was, "I got you Neisha Boo." Then I closed my eyes again.

She grabbed my dick with both hands and slowly put it in her mouth.

"Just remember, no teeth, all lips and tongue. Just do whatever feels natural." I coached.

After 5 minutes of coaching Laneisha had it down pat. I mean, it turned out to be close to the best head I ever had. I could tell that she was doing it just to please me. I was pleased!

When I felt myself about to cum, I stopped her and controlled myself. I would have usually busted in a broad's throat, but deep down inside I really want to knock her little ass up. So, I'm saving it all up to put inside of her pussy. I'm foul, I know it!

I pulled her up and had her get on her hands and knees on the edge of the bed while I stood up behind her. Her body tensed as I put one hand on the small of her back to adjust her body to the perfect angle. I slowly guided myself into her tight, wet pussy and immediately felt the warmness of her walls that I was tweaking for. Once I finally got all the way inside of her, she was grabbing the sheets like she was trying to tear open the mattress. So, I started off slow, but with long strokes.

"It hurts, Jakill, but don't stop! Don't stop! Don't stop!" Laneisha screamed into the pillow that she had begun biting on.

So, I speeded up the pace and put more force into my thrusts. She looked back at me and had tears coming down her face. Tears of pain and joy at the same time.

That made me get into it even more.

"Whose pussy is this. Neisha Boo?" I asked while smacking her on her ass a couple times.

"Yours, Jakill! Yours and only yours, baby!"

I busted at the sound of that.

I dicked, her down for another hour or so, and we fell asleep cuddled up.

I got up at 7:45 a.m. and woke up Laneisha so that we could take a quick shower before we bounce, when she walked into the bathroom, I grabbed my SIM card and called D-Slug to make sure that he was up.

"Yeah, cuz, I'm up." D said while Mia was moaning in the background.

I started laughing and hung up. I walked into the bathroom, still naked from last night, and got in the shower with her. We knew that we didn't have enough time to finish whatever we start. So, after a few touches, a quick shower, and freshening up, we met D-Slug and Mia in the lobby and then left.

"Usually, ya'll know we would be going to go get some breakfast at Scotty's or somewhere." I said when we got into my car, "but me and D got to handle somethin in a couple minutes. I can drop ya'll off at the diner and give ya'll a couple dollars for the bill and a jitney, or I can take y'all home." I gave them the option.

"You can drop us off at Scotty's cause you definitely made me work up an appetite." Laneisha said and her and Mia giggled.

We dropped them off and I gave Laneisha $100. Then we headed straight to Butch's crib.

"I was thinkin last night either Jeff Rose or Tim Murphy." I said and looked at D-Slug to let him know that I was dead serious.

"Oh, we goin after the big dogs now, huh?"

"If its dog eat dog, why keep biting pups? Feel me?" I said more than asked. *"I made up my mind though. We gettin Jeff tomorrow night, cuz. Fuck it."*

"We gonna have to catch him coming home on the late-night cause you know he be having all his flunkies with him." He suggested.

"Naw. I got a better idea. We gonna catch him at his store and put his bitch ass in the trunk. You know he don't like niggas round his store. So, we'll catch him tonight solo before he closes up."

"You already know I'm bout whatever. Is we slumpin this nigga too?" D-Slug asked excitedly.

I looked at D like that was the stupidest question

that he could have asked. "Either him or eventually us. You know how the game go, cuz. More birds, more bodies, nigga."

"Yeah, nigga. More birds, more bodies. I fuck with that." D-Slug said as we turned on to Butch's street.

CHAPTER 10

We pulled up at Butch's spot, and just like yesterday, he was rocking back and forth on his heels, waiting for his $300. He got in and we drove to McMurray Township.

We pulled up at the dealership and I noticed that the Lexus in the front was now replaced by a black on black BMW. Dave spotted us and ran over to me.

"Hey, buddy. You're back already. What's wrong?" Dave asked confused.

"Nothing. That's why I'm back. My cuz," I said and looked at D-Slug, "is trying to cop something nice." I replied.

We walked up to the top lot and as soon as D-Slug saw the royal blue Mustang 5.0, with the white drop top, white leather interior, tinted windows, and chrome 100 spoke Dayton rims. He was hooked.

Dave then did the same routine that he used on me, and just like with me it wasn't even necessary. He guided us to the trunk of the car. "This trunk is not like yours, but it's close enough." Dave looked at me and said as he opened the trunk.

D's eyes almost popped out of his head at the sight of his about to be sounds. "This the shit right here, cuz." D- Slug said and rubbed his beardless chin.

It was 4 12" JBL subs built into a box that covered the small trunk.

Dave smiled. "There's four seven-hundred-watt amps and two dual hundred-watt cross-overs hidden under the box." He informed us.

"This is me." D whispered to himself.

Dave cleared his throat to get D's attention. "Since your boy, JD, here just put some C-Notes in my pockets yesterday. I'll put you behind the wheel of this for forty-five hundred. Nothing more, nothing less."

"Let's get it." D-Slug immediately responded without any negotiation.

After the paperwork was completed, D gave Butch $300 and Butch got in my car and continuously counted the money repeatedly while me and D were still standing in front of his new 5.0.

"I'm bout to drop off Butch and then chef that coke up. I got a plan for that too." I said to D-Slug as he was getting into his new car. I doubt that he was paying me any attention at that moment.

He adjusted his seats and fucked with every knob in the car. "Fill me in later, cuz. Right now. I'm bout to go shit on a few mufuckers. Let me get a couple CD's though till I hit Dorsey's Record's spot." D-Slug said and continued fucking with everything in his sight.

I gave him a couple CD's out of my car and then we both peeled off.

"Yo, Butch." I said while we were driving back to Homiwood. "Do you know how to cook up?"

Without removing the Newport from his lips, he said, "I know how to cook up and cop, lil nigga." We both laughed as the Newport never fell.

I cut my laughing short. "I'm trying to hire you as a chef if you good with it." I said. I honked my horn at a group of young broads walking down the Ave. I continued, "I'm a drop you off and come right back with some work to see what you can do. If it's right, I got you."

"What's my salary gonna be then?"

"Five hunnit every byrd. Plus, whatever bubbles."

Butch's eyes got big as possible.

"Just don't soda my shit so you can keep more." I

said letting him know that I'm on to all the tricks. "If it ain't 'Al' ya fired."

"Sounds good to me, lil nigga." He said anticipating his new job.

We pulled up at his crib. "I'll be back in ten minutes," I said as Butch got out of my car.

"I'll be here."

I'm sure you will be, I thought as I pulled off.

I drove straight to the cut crib. E-Wok was the only nigga there, but he was passed out on the couch. So, I crept down to the stash and grabbed one of the birds. I put the work on the table then crept back into the living room to make sure that Wokky was still asleep. It's not that I don't trust him, it's just that he's not one of my closest niggas and also you know how those real crispy black niggas always look like they're up to some sneaky shit.

Once I peeped that Wokky was asleep I went into the kitchen and got 2 Giant Eagle grocery store bags. I took the bags to the living room table. I eyeballed a quarter byrd. I put the remaining 3 quarters in one of the bags and then back into the stash. I then looked at the quarter on the table again to make sure that it looked about right.

I got to jack a nigga for a scale, I thought and

laughed to myself.

I put the quarter in the other bag and dipped back to Butch's crib.

When I walked into Butch's crib, this motherfucker had on a fucking apron, a Newport hanging out of his mouth, and Al Green playing out of the stereo low as fuck. You couldn't tell him that he wasn't back in his prime right now. Fiends are funny as hell!

Butch did some type of little dance where he slid one foot to the side and flapped his arms like a bird. "Yeah, lil nigga. I used to re-up and turn Al on. Boy, I was the best chef in Allegheny County. I could turn whatever into whatever and still have the best shit around," Butch campaigned.

"I believe you and all that," I said as I tossed him the bag, "but just make sure my shit is the best you ever cooked, and I'll have more for you."

He slid again, spun around, and then headed to the kitchen with the work.

I laughed as I sat down on a milk crate with a pillow on top of it. There was one couch in that living room, but it looked like it survived 10 fires and a knife fight, so the crate was the best option.

"Got my mind right and the Chopper held tight/ Nigga let me know wutz smackin 2night.

I barely heard my phone but A1 happened to take a breath for a split second. I looked at the Caller ID and instantly realized that I haven't talked to Kia since yesterday.

"Kia, what's up, love?" I asked hoping that she wasn't mad.

"Hey, baby. I miss you. How's my daddy doing?" Kia asked in her sexy voice like nothing was wrong.

"I'm good. My fault I ain't hit you up last night but I had a crazy ass migraine." I used my emergency excuse. She knows that I really get migraines, so it's always a believable excuse.

"Awe. Are you cool now, baby?" She asked concerned.

Two roaches ran down the arm of the couch. *I'm glad I knew better than to sit there,* I thought.

"You know ya voice cures anything, Kia."

"Boy, I swear I'm the luckiest woman in the world."

"Well, I'm bout to make you luckier. If you could have any car what would it be?" I asked.

"Probably a Benz or a Lexus. I don't know. Why, is

you gonna get me one for Christmas?" She joked.

I couldn't help but to think how Laneisha would have probably said a Honda Civic or something cheap just to get around in.

"Maybe," I responded.

We bullshitted on the phone for a minute until Butch was done cooking. Then I told Kia that I would call her later on.

"It's gonna be wet for a minute, lil nigga, but I still got it," Butch said and then excitedly put his hand in the air to give me a "high 5" like he had just hit the game winning shot at the buzzer.

Butch then walked over to the mantle and poured us cups of Thunderbird. Then he walked back over, handed me a cup, then sat down on the couch like he wanted to talk.

Before Butch could start his "I used to" stories, I took a gulp of the Thunderbird and called Dave the car dealer.

"McMurray's New and Used. This is Dave. What can I sell you?"

"This is JD." I said.

"If you are trying to buy another car I might just

give it to you for free this time," Dave said, then quickly added, "No, I'm joking. But you are contributing to Little Davey's college fund."

We both laughed at the truth.

I took a big gulp of the Thunderbird. "Listen, I wasn't payin attention, but do you got any new Benz's," I asked hesitantly.

"How new are you talking?"

"New, new. Like never been drove more than a mile new."

"Hold on a sec, JD," Dave said and sat the phone down.

I heard him ask a couple people in the background.

He got back on the phone. "Buddy, you're in luck. A brand new CLK320 just came in a few minutes ago. It's nice and all, but I'm going to be honest with you, it's more of a girly car. I can order you the," he was saying until I cut him off.

"Yeah, that's what I need. It's for my woman," I said thinking about his girly vs. manly sales pitch. "How much?"

Dave paused for a few seconds. "If it's cash, give me thirty-five large, and that's a steal," he replied.

I took 2 big gulps from my cup.

"Aight listen, I'm getting it for my girl right, and I want to get it in her name, but how do we go bout that without thirty-five stacks gettin me on The World's Dumbest Criminals?" I asked, and Dave laughed like I wasn't dead ass serious.

"Buddy, buddy. First and foremost, if you can't trust your car dealer, who can you trust? We both know that Butch Franklin is not really your uncle, but I didn't and don't care. Like you, I'm in the business of making money. My dad owns the joint, so I pretty much run everything. Including the paperwork. Just come in and we'll talk then. Oh, I almost forgot, does she have insurance, because if not, she can get it right across the street at the Allstate Agency."

"Yeah, that's good lookin. We'll be there on Saturday at my regular time. Can you have a bow tied around it or am I askin too much?"

"Consider it done, buddy, and I'll have it washed right before you get here. I'll see you Saturday. Great doing business with you, JD," he said, and we hung up.

Butch got up and walked out on the porch when he seen me begin dialing another number.

"Neisha Boo, what's smackin, sexy?" I asked when she answered the phone.

"Baby, I was just thinking about you. You know D came up here acting like a donkey and picked up Mia. I don't know who put it on who last night. Mia was talking about him all morning and then he come pick her up as soon as he bought his car," Laneisha said.

"You know you was the first woman in my car soon as I bought it," I said and drank the rest of the Thunderbird.

"Yeah, I know. And you know it is what it is," she said sounding sexy as last night.

"And it always will be," I responded.

We talked on the phone for a while about everything. We talked about life, our families, D-Slug and Mia, her birthday coming up on Halloween, and she even put me on to her plans to go to Pitt next year for college. This conversation was different than me and Kia's conversations because it was going both ways and I didn't feel obligated to stay on the phone. Plus, Laneisha was more interested in talking about me and not her. We talked and talked until Butch tapped me on my shoulder.

"It's ready as it's gonna get, lil nigga," he said like he

had a coke cooking timer in his head, then walked into the kitchen.

"Neisha Boo, let me hit you back," I said into the phone and ended the conversation.

I walked into the kitchen and saw Butch smiling from ear to ear. He waved his hand over the work like he just served stuffed duck at a country club.

"What's it hittin for?" I asked.

"Let's find out."

He grabbed about a dime piece of crack and walked out on the porch with me following him. Vita was standing across the street clucking. Butch called her over to us.

"Baby, I got somethin for you. Here, take this and go in the bathroom. Let me know how it taste," Butch said and Vita snatched the crack out of his hand.

Minutes later Vita came back down the steps beaming bad.

"Butchy, you got some more of that or what? That's that meltdown right there, baby. Who you get that shit off?" Vita asked excitedly like it couldn't have been me with it.

She's probably wondering if somebody would trick with her ugly ass so that she could get some of this new meltdown, I thought. "Come around Hale in a minute and all the niggas will have it. And we bringin back the original size dubs. Fuck that small shit... As long as you come straight though," I said matter of factly.

Vita ran off the porch without saying a word, probably to round up her squad and ante up.

I gave Butch $125 and told him that I would be back around 8 PM so that he could chef up some more work.

Butch's face lit up. "I'll be here, lil nigga."

I hopped in my ride with the Chopper in the trunk that had who-knows how many bodies on it, and 9 zips of crack right next to it. Good thing I'm only going right around the corner, I thought.

When I pulled up in front of the cut crib E-Wok and Boo walked down off the porch and approached my car.

"What's up, cuz?" Boo asked as Wokky just gave me a head nod.

"Ain't shit. But I need ya'll to find the rest of the niggas. I need ya'll to drag them out of some pussy if you got to and be back here in an hour," I said and paused for a second. "If not, that's ya'll lost."

They quickly scattered like we were playing Release The Den and I was "it" or some shit.

Once they were out of sight, I took the work out of the trunk and went in the cut crib. I walked into the dining room and put the work on the table. Then I called D- Slug.

"D, where you at?" I asked into the phone.

"Ridin through East Lib with Mia." He replied.

"Oh, that's ya new Boo Butt, huh?" I joked.

"Cuz," is all that he could say.

"Look, we got an important meeting jumpin off at the cut crib in an hour, cuz. I need you here cause it's comin from both of us. Drop Mia off for a lil bit."

"Got you. I'll be through in a second."

"I'm out," I said and hung up.

I walked into the living room and turned on the James Bond game so that I could sharpen my skills for the next bet. I ended up losing almost every game because Kia had called me as soon as I started and we talked the entire time until all the niggas, except D-Slug, arrived.

The niggas were all standing around, quiet, trying to figure out what was so important. They all had different looks on their faces. Wokky was looking like he already knew, but I knew that he had no idea.

"Soon as D get here, we got to holla at ya'll bout some real shit," I said right before D-Slug walked into the crib.

D looked around at everybody. "What I miss?" He asked.

"Nothing," I replied as I stood up and began walking into the hallway. "Let's go in the dining room for a minute."

They all followed me through the hallway.

"What's this bout, cuz?" Teeke whispered to Boo.

"I'm bout to find out with you, nigga." Boo whispered back as we walked through the dining room door.

Once inside the room I sat in the chair at the head of the table. D-Slug naturally sat at the other end. Boo sat directly at my right. Mayo sat on my left. Gizzle sat on top of an old broke floor model TV behind D-Slug. The rest of the niggas were standing around us.

I had already thought of how I was going to say what I planned on saying.

I looked at D-Slug and then at Big Hurt.

"Aight look, everybody's throwin up The Tre, reppin the block and shit, but if we all gonna be reppin the same block, we gotta be reppin each other." I said and paused to make sure that all the niggas were paying attention. Once I was positive that they were, I continued, "We all gotta be organized and eatin. As y'all can see by the rides out front, me and D is aight. It ain't cool though cause ya'll, our niggas, ain't right," I was saying until E-Wok interrupted me.

"What you gettin at, cuz?" E-Wok impatiently asked.

Boo meanmugged him. "Damn, let the nigga say what he was sayin and find out," Boo said.

"Like I was sayin though. I want us to be like how Cora was back in the day. How Sterrett Street was before Teddy told on all of them. And how the Seventy-Six was. I want us to be like that but better. To the point that them niggas hear bout us and be like 'I wish we would have been like them Hale Street niggas.' Feel me?" I asked and looked around at everybody nodding their heads in agreement. I continued, "We got what it takes to do it. We all thorough niggas, and I know everybody got guns. Hopefully, everybody will bust em when it comes time to. But I'm gonna put a Chopper under the couch in the living room to protect the fort. This," I looked around, "is the fuckin fort, niggas."

I picked up the bag and dumped all the crack on top

of the table. At that very moment, all niggas' eyes lit up.

Mayo looked at me, back to the work, then back at me. "What you doin with all this cuz?" He asked.

I pushed the crack farther away from me on the table. "Naw, what is y'all doin with this?" I responded.

Niggas were looking around at each other as they tried to decipher exactly what I meant by that. While they were trying to figure it out, I stood up and began separating the work into what appeared to be 9 equal piles—1 ounce in each pile.

I got to jack a nigga for a scale, I thought as I put the 9 piles onto 9 plates and scooted 7 plates in front of all the niggas, who were now all standing up around the table. They all stood in silence and waited for me to speak again.

"Aight, peep game. Me and D is givin all y'all a zip of melt, and I mean givin. We don't want shit back, but here's the conditions: you gotta cop off me and D, nobody else. You can't cop less that what we givin you right now. It's eight hunnit a zip, and ya dubs gotta be boulders, so we can bring all the clucks back to the Eastside of the hood. And if you get booked... you know the rest." I said and looked at D-Slug.

"If y'all take this shit right now, that's what y'all

acceptin with it." D-Slug added. He looked at all the niggas standing there and continued, "All we doin is putting y'all on for free."

"That's what I'm talkin bout, cuz," Boo said and slowly turned the plate in front of him 180°.

"Let's get it," Teeke said excitedly.

"We bout to be on top. Believe that," said Daz.

"I'm with it three hunnit percent, cuz" Big Hurt said in between deep breaths.

Mayo looked at me and said, "Nigga, I would have to be stupid to turn that down. Shit."

E-Wok and Gizzle both just silently nodded their heads, probably thinking about what cars that they were going to buy.

"If yall fuck up y'all flip, that's on y'all," I said with an extremely serious tone. "Now get some baggies and go get that scrilla. Vita's already puttin the word out that we got that meltdown. A couple niggas on each corner and we'll smash em. Everybody gotta get cell phones too. Mufuckas got the internet on their phone's and this nigga got a fuckin pager. It probably ain't even got the time on it." I said, and everybody looked at Daz's pager sitting on the table in front of him and we all laughed.

"I feel you. I feel you," Daz said and laughed himself.

"Everybody got me and D's numbers. I need y'all to roll out, so I can holla at D and Boo for a minute," I said and ushered all of the rest of them to the door once they put their crack into the baggies.

After a few "good looks", a couple "I'll hollas" and a couple of pounds I walked back into the dining room, where D-Slug and Boo were silently sitting, waiting to hear what else I had planned.

"What up, y'all?" Boo finally asked curiously.

"Me and D know you got that hunger, cuz. You got it more than the rest of the niggas," I said.

"Yeah, and we want you to be right," D-Slug said, still trying to figure out where I was going with this conversation.

"So, what's up?" asked Boo.

"Take this other zip too on the strength," I slid another plate to him and continued, "and take this zip right here, give half to Hurt and I want you to use the other half for samples." I slid the last plate in front of him. "Go to all the spots and just give that shit away. Dig me?"

"Tell all the smokers it's that Hale Street meltdown.

That'll bring money to the block, but especially to you since you the one that gave em that free shit. Ya know?" D asked.

"Yeah, I'm with you. Good lookin, my niggas," Boo gratefully replied.

"Aight, grab that and get ya money. I gotta holla at JD real quick," D-Slug said and stood up.

As soon as Boo left D-Slug looked at me and said, "You got a real fuckin masterplan, nigga."

I pounded him up. "No, nigga, we got a fuckin masterplan. Ain't shit change at all, cuz."

"I want to know if that lick is still on for tomorrow though?" D asked.

I laughed. "No question. I need that bad too. I'm gettin Kia a fuckin Benz on Saturday. I already got Dave holdin it for me."

"Sucka for love ass nigga," D-Slug said and started laughing.

"Nigga, but you handcuffed Lil Mia out of all the freaks," I responded.

"Hold up though. I only put the cuffs around her neck. Niggas can have the titties down," he said and we both laughed. "Matter of fact," he continued, "I'm bout to go get her right now and hit the Telly. Is you grabbin up Laneisha?"

I rubbed my hands together. "Naw, cuz. I'm takin some more work to Butch's kitchen. I gotta plan this lick out too. Tell Laneisha I'm a call her in a lil bit and make her feel special," I said and pounded him up again.

"I got you. Holla at me if somethin come up," D-Slug said as he walked out of the dining room door to leave.

I waited a few minutes and then walked into the living room to make sure that nobody had come back into the crib. After I made sure that there were no watchers, I walked down into the basement and grabbed 1 and 3/4 birds out of the stashspot, along with one of the Choppers and a banana clip. I sat at the dining room table and spent some time loading up the clip and thinking about a lick. Once all of the bullets were in the clip, I put the Chopper under the couch like I said that I would for the niggas.

I walked back into the living room, grabbed the bag that contained the work and walked out of the crib. Big Hurt was the only nigga standing directly in front of his crib hustlin. The rest of the niggas were all spaced out on opposite corners. I gave him a pound and hopped in my

Iroc Z.

When I got to Butch's house it was like he was waiting on me, which he probably was doing. He had the Al Green pounding, the apron on, and I swear he had the very same Newport hanging out of his mouth.

Butch had a new dance for me this time though. Instead of sticking to his old school shit, he tried to do the little dance that Dame Dash be doing in all Jay-Z's videos but ended up looking like he was arm-wrestling and losing. I held my laugh in so that I wouldn't have to hear any of his back in the day stories.

"Ready, lil nigga?" Butch asked without letting the cigarette fall from his lip.

"Let's get it smackin," I said and tossed him the bag.

While Butch was doing what he was getting paid to do I called Kia for a very short amount of time, Laneisha for a while, and fell asleep sitting on the crate with my head leaning against the dirty ass wall behind me. I was down for the count for a minute dreaming about money until Butch shook me by my shoulder and screamed that "the house is on fire."

I jumped up, feeling like I was in a hood version of *The Twilight Zone*. I cleared the clouds out of my head and quickly realized that I was just in a crackhead's crib and Butch was just fucking with me about the fire just to wake me up.

"Do I still got it or what?" He asked, doing his "I got some ice cream" dance like he was 5 years old.

I wiped my eyes with my hands. I grabbed the bag out of his hands, looked in it, and saw that I was asleep long enough for him to finish all of the work.

"Yo, cuz, let me give you the eight and some change tomorrow night. Aight. That's cool?" I said more than asked.

He knew that he had no choice. "That's cool, lil nigga. You the boss," he replied and made me feel uncomfortable with that title.

I stood up and headed to the door. "I'm a holla at you tomorrow. Make sure mufuckas know where that melt is," I said as I walked down the porch steps.

Now I'm back in my ride with close to 2 birds of crack, a dirty Chopper, and I still ain't got no scale yet, I thought. I took the work to the cut crib through the back alley so that hopefully none of the niggas would peep me.

I walked in the backdoor of the cut crib and bumped directly into E-Wok, who was behind the door getting a frying pan out from the bottom cupboard.

"Damn, cuz, you scared the shit out me," E-Wok said clearly shaken up.

"How is you shaking in our own fuckin fort?" I asked jokingly.

He looked in the direction of the living room. "Cause the Chopper you left is all the way in there and I'm in here with nothing."

It didn't take him long to check to see if I had put that gun under the couch already, I thought.

"What you bout to cook though?" I asked starvingly.

"Burgers."

"Hook me up, cuz," I said as I walked into the dining room.

I figured that Wokky was too busy trying to take care of his munchies to pay any attention to me going into the basement, so I took the work down the steps and stashed it in the spot. I walked back upstairs and went straight into the living room. I intended on playing a video game until the food was done but I yawned one too many times and thought about the comfortable money getting dreamland that I was just in at Butch's crib and fell asleep before I even cut the game on. E-Wok didn't even wake me up either. Big Hurt must have eaten my food cause I heard him come in and start playing Madden with E-Wok all night while I was asleep.

CHAPTER 11

"JD! JD! Cuz, wake up," Boo screamed in my ear.

"What time is it?" I asked half expecting it to be in the middle of the night.

"It's a lil after seven in the morning and there's scrilla everywhere."

"What the fuck is you wakin me up this early in the morning for then?" I asked a little angry.

"I need to flip. I got it smackin out there still. All the niggas dipped off like midnight. I been killin em all night, cuz," Boo said and patted his pockets.

I jumped right up. "What you need?" I asked already getting up off the run-down couch.

E-Wok was laying on the floor in front of the TV and managed to stay sleep through Boo's screaming. Hurt must have went upstairs, I though as I looked around.

"Just give me three zips."

"That's it? I know you ain't blow the rest of ya change that quick?" I asked about to get a little disappointed in him.

He looked at me like I was crazy. "Naw. I'm a cop an eighty next flip," he said referring to 4½ ounces. "I had to at least start stashin some scrill for a lawyer."

"I knew you had it in you, cuz," I said and let out a light laugh. "Aight peep, let me use the bathroom real quick and then I'm a go get it for you. I'll be back in like ten minutes. Tell em to hold on."

Boo turned around and ran out of the house at the thought of getting ready to blow up. As soon as he was out of the crib, I peeped that E-Wok was still asleep, so I crept downstairs and grabbed a couple chunks of crack in my bare hands. Then I ran into the kitchen a got a couple of baggies from in the drawer. I quickly walked to the bathroom and put about 3 zips of crack into the baggies. I put the 3 zips into my pockets and put the left-over crack back into the stash in the basement. I noticed that E-Wok was still asleep on the floor, but facing a different direction, as I walked out of the front door.

Boo was standing in front of the cut crib, letting all the smokers know that he was about to re-up shortly. I gave him a head nod as I walked past him to get into my car, letting him know that I was on my way, allegedly, to pick up his PK.

I got in my car and sped off. I drove around the hood for a second, just thinking about how I'm going to have to get another cut crib just to stash the work at when me and D-Slug be on top of the world. I wonder if Wokky was eye-hustlin when I thought he was asleep, I wondered. Then I thought about how I'm also going to have to get a safe in the spot I'm getting with Kia.

After 5 minutes of driving and thinking I went back to the block. Boo ran to my car as soon as I pulled up. He even opened my door for me before I put the car in park. I took him side of the cut crib through the backdoor, just in case E-Wok or Big Hurt was awake.

Once inside, I gave Boo the baggies of crack and he had exactly $2,400 for me in wrinkled and crumbled up bills. The only words that were exchanged after the transaction was when Boo told me that he'll holla at me as soon as he need to flip again, right before he ran out of the backdoor in full speed.

I got in my car and dipped to my mom's crib. I knew that she was a work, so instead of me running straight to my room I went into the kitchen and put 4 microwavable sausage, egg, and cheese biscuits into the microwave. Then went up to my room and put the money that I got from Boo inside of the wall, but on a different ledge than the lawyer fee. I then laid down on the bed, for what I believed would only be for a few minutes and fell asleep.

When I woke up 2 hours later, I was happy that I had put my breakfast in the microwave and not the oven like I usually do. I ate my cold sandwiches and spent most of the rest of the day in the crib talking to the usual suspects on the phone about the same shit as always and plotting on Jeff Rose.

Throughout the day though I had to hit the block a couple of times so the niggas could re-up. Daz, Teeke, and Mayo all copped 2 zips a piece. Gizzle got 1½ zips. Hurt and Wokky both copped a lonely zip. I ended up taking the byrd of coke, the byrd of crack, and $7,600 with me back to my mom's crib. I left the remaining 16½ zips in the stashspot at the cut crib though. I don't know what it is, but I been feeling a little paranoid like somebody is plotting on me, and that's why I took a majority of the work with me. I guess all the shit I been doing is catching up to my mind.

I put all the money that I had got from them niggas inside of the wall of the same ledge where I had put Boo's money. This is the "flip fee" ledge, I said to myself and smiled at how the plan is coming together perfectly. Then I put the work in a couple of shoe boxes under my bed with the rest of my kicks.

"Got my mind right and the Chopper held tight, Nigga let me know wutz smacking 2night."

"What's smackin, D?" I answered after I looked at the Caller ID.

"Yo, cuz some of Spade's punk ass niggas came around here a couple minutes ago dumpin out they ride and shit," D-Slug calmly said like nothing happened.

"Is nigga cool?"

"Hell yeah! Nigga, I'm glad you remembered to put the Chopper under the couch. Me and Boo out here bustin at their shit with a four-nickle and a Glock then Teeke came out the spot lettin the Chopper go crazy. I don't think he hit shit though. TK kind of reminded me of the way you were bustin at bitch ass Black back in the day," he clowned and started laughing.

I felt a meanmug form on my face. "Any other nigga would get it for that cuz," I said angrily about his little joke.

D knew that I wasn't as mad at him as much as I tried to make it sound.

"I'm just fuckin with you, JD. What's up with that

situation though? You know it's close to that time."

I walked over to the radio and turned on 50Cent's *Get Rich Or Die Trying* CD. "Do you still got Daz's mom's car parked in the cut?" I asked as the song *"Many Men"* played.

"Yeah. Why? What's up?"

"Grab ya Chopper out the stash. Put ya ride in the cut and pick me up at my mom's spot in Daz's mom's shit." I responded.

"Right now?" D-Slug asked confused.

"Yeah, cuz. It's time," I said and hung up.

I hurried up and put on a pair of black Dickie's pants and a black T-shirt as usual. D-Slug was out front honking the horn by the time I got the shirt over my head. *He's tweakin for this lick as bad as I am.* I thought.

After D picked me up, we rode around as I drank some vodka and he smoked some dro until 8:30 p.m.

When I saw what time, it was I grabbed the bag that I brought with me off the back seat. "Let's get it smackin, nigga," I said and patted the bag.

"What you got?" D-Slug asked curiously.

"Duct tape and a couple pair of handcuffs. Pull up in front of the store and we gonna hop right out and run up in there. Pat him down and handcuff him behind his back. And duct tape his mouth and ankles. That nigga can hop to the trunk. If anybody else in there, we gonna take their phones and handcuff em to anything that'll hold em for a minute. You got it, cuz?"

D-Slug sat there and looked at me with a look that let me know that he did not expect me to have this lick planned out this much. He probably thought that we would just wait on him to come out and hope shit go right.

"Got it," is all D said as we pulled up directly in front of the store.

I took a quick gulp of vodka. We put on our masks and gloves, then was out of the car and inside of the store in a matter of a few seconds. Luckily, it's a dark street with trees along the sidewalk so nobody saw us.

D-Slug was ahead of me as we ran inside. There was an old lady with her back to us, buying toilet paper, and didn't even turn around to see what was about to go down in her presence. Jeff, however, seen the Choppers immediately and froze up like a pure bitch.

D ran up to Jeff and put his Chopper to Jeff's neck. "Don't say shit, you bitch ass nigga," D-slug said.

The old lady quickly turned around and got the

surprise of her life.

"Stay calm. We ain't gonna hurt you," I assured her in a calm tone. "Just let me handcuff you to that pipe so there won't be any problems."

I walked her over to the sink and handcuffed her to a pipe that was under it.

"Don't move or I'm a kill you, nigga," D said to Jeff.

I turned around and saw D-Slug patting down Jeff and it reminded me that I had to pat down this lady too.

"Don't be scared but I got to check you for a phone," I said to her.

The old lady still didn't scream or even say a single word. I guess she already knew that this was going to happen to somebody in this store one day.

I went through the small purse and quickly came across a Boost Mobile. Then I walked over to behind the counter where D had Jeff handcuffed at the wrists and duct tape across his mouth and around his ankles. I immediately noticed that D was now holding a Desert Eagle in his right hand and his Chopper were hanging from a rope around his neck. He must have got that burner off Jeff, I realized.

D-Slug peeped me staring at the Desert Eagle. "I got his phone too, cuz," he said.

Jeff was standing there sweating like he had just played 10 games of ball in a row. The look on his face let me know that Jeff was pretty sure that he was going to die tonight. The look in my eyes probably let him know that he was right.

I cut off the lights before me and D-Slug hopped Jeff to the trunk, closing the door behind us. I told myself to remember to call the pigs after our lick so that they could free that old lady, but I got to make sure that I do it in a way that won't lead back to me or D.

Jeff attempted to struggle to not get inside of the trunk, but after D hit him with his own gun in the head several times, he reluctantly climbed in.

D-Slug took the wheel again and managed to hit every single bump and pothole he could find in the street, just to make Jeff's last ride that much more unpleasant. It took us 10 minutes to pull up in Jeff's back driveway to his 3 floors, pool in the back, stuntastic crib in Penn Hills. Not only did he have the Benz that he kept parked on Cora Street, but he also had 2 white Benz's parked in the driveway. I immediately knew that they were "his and hers."

"You ready, cuz?" D-Slug asked to snap me out of

my analysis bag.

"No question," I replied as we both got out of the car at the same time.

We walked around the car to the trunk. I took a deep breath before I opened it. Jeff leaned his head up and saw the place that he had already knew we would end up.

"Get ya bitch ass out the trunk, nigga." D-Slug demanded as he grabbed Jeff by his shirt collar and drug him out of the trunk onto the ground.

Jeff grunted as he hit the ground on his face and shoulder.

"How many mufuckas is in the crib right now?" I asked and took the tape off his mouth with one pull that made him squint his eyes.

To my surprise Jeff didn't scream as most niggas would have. "Just my girl and my baby. Don't hurt them, cuz." He pleaded, sounding as if he was going to cry.

D grabbed Jeff by his collar again and pulled it as tight around Jeff's neck as possible. "As long as we get the scrilla and coke," D-Slug lied.

D-Slug helped Jeff get to his feet and we hopped him a few steps until D got tired of that and picked Jeff up over his shoulder. D carried Jeff down the rest of the long pathway past the Nomads to the backdoor, while holding his Chopper in one hand poking Jeff in his ribs the entire time. I was walking behind them with my Chopper aimed at the door just in case somebody in the crib saw us and came up with some type of stupid idea to be a dead hero. I also had to keep my eyes on the woods that covered the spacious backyard.

We got to the door and I quickly walked around them and pulled out Jeff's keys, which D-Slug took from him during his pat down. I showed Jeff each key until he told me which one would open the door. I opened the door and we walked directly into the kitchen at the same time as his broad, who was coming to greet him completely naked. She the surprise of her life when she saw D- Slug dropping Jeff to the ground on his side. Before she could say a word, I ran over to her and put the barrel of my Chopper in her mouth deep enough to take out her tonsils.

"Don't scream, bitch," I demanded her.

She whimpered and attempted to cover up her big chocolate titties with her small hands. She began to tremble in fear.

Jeff saw his broad's fear and calmly said to her, "Baby, just chill. They ain't gonna hurt you. Just be quiet and once I give them what they want they'll be out of here."

I'm sure that she didn't believe him, but his words calmed her down a little bit.

D-Slug put his gun to the side of Jeff's head. "Good nigga. Now take us to what we want then," D-Slug said, clearly growing impatient.

Jeff hopped and guided us into the laid out living room that was bigger than my mom's living room and dining room combined. There was a white soft leather wrap around couch that had to be the longest couch I had ever seen. He even had a big ass entertainment center built into the wall. This is gonna be my crib one day, I thought as Jeff walked to a large picture hanging on the wall.

"It's behind that," Jeff informed us.

Me and D-Slug looked at each other amazed.

"What, you think you Scarface or somebody nigga? What's the combination?" I asked Jeff while holding my burner to his broad's stomach.

D-Slug put his Chopper to Jeff's side, and he began to run down the number as I punched them into the digital lock on the safe. Once it clicked open, I pushed Jeff's broad back and ordered her to sit down on the couch. She obeyed quietly. Jeff gave her a look of assurance even though he knew this would more than likely be his last few minutes breathing.

I couldn't believe my eyes as I looked into the large safe. Half of the safe was coke and the other half was money. Everything was in perfect piles and stacks from the front to the back.

I looked at Jeff and grinned. "Better us than the jakes, nigga." I said, and D did his sinister laugh. Then I looked at his broad and threw her the bag. "Put every fuckin think in the bag, bitch."

I wasn't worried about her pulling any slick shit because I had scanned the safe to make sure that there wasn't a burner in there off top. Ever since Spade I will make that number one on our to do list every time that a safe get opened. I guess Jeff knew that that would never work too.

She quickly got up and started scooping everything out of the safe and into the bag hoping that the faster she moved, the faster we would be out of her crib.

I grabbed the bag out of her hands when she was done and looked into the safe to make sure that she didn't try to keep anything. It was all in the bag. Then I pushed his broad back onto the couch.

"Cuz, you ready to go?" I asked D-Slug, giving him the hint that he was waiting for.

Without any hesitation, D filled Jeff Rose up with Chopper bullets until there was pieces of him everywhere. His broad began screaming for help as loud as possible.

I quickly jumped on top of Jeff broad's naked frame and put my knees on her shoulders so that she couldn't move. Then I leaned over and grabbed the duct tape out of the bag. I wrapped the duct tape around her entire face, only leaving her nose uncovered. After she was nearly inaudible, I taped her ankles and dragged her over to the steps and handcuffed her to the railing. D- Slug was following behind me trying to get a peek at her shaved pussy. She kept her legs squeezed together tightly assuming me and D were going to rape her.

Even though we both got peeks at her pussy, we never had any intentions of taking any pussy. That was nowhere near that she would even think that, but then I had to realize that we had her tied up naked right after slumping her nigga—what broad would think anything other than that?

Once ol girl was secured to the railing me and D-

Slug ran out of the crib the same way we entered. We got into the car and peeled off. My heart was still pounding in my chest from the adrenaline rush. D was breathing heavy and didn't even notice it as we sped back to the hood.

We were both completely silent, listening for sirens, until we got to the beginning of the hood.

"Yo, I know I didn't see how much I think I seen in that safe?" D-Slug asked for reassurance.

I looked at the bag on the backseat and then at D-Slug. "D, we got to go to my mom's crib with this shit. Pull up in the back."

We parked in the driveway and ran into the crib. I had the duffle bag over my shoulder as we walked past my mom's room on the way to my room. She just looked up from her bed through the cracked door and shook her head as usual. D spoke and got no response. I kept it moving.

Once we got into my room, I told D-Slug to whisper just in case my mom was earhustlin. I turned on Three Six Mafia's CD low because I was paranoid that my mom could still hear our whispers.

While I was turning on the sounds D grabbed the bag and emptied it out on the bed, and it seemed like the contents just kept pouring. D grabbed a couple dollars and threw them in the air to make it rain like all niggas claim that they be doing.

I walked to the bed and grabbed a couple dollars just to smell them. The money was all wrapped in rubber band stacks, and all the bills were crispy like he ironed them.

"There's definitely a Money God. cuz," I said to D as I reached to pick up a byrd of powder.

D quickly kneeled at the side of the bed, folded his hands, closed his eyes, and said, "Dear Money God, thank you for all of the bitch ass niggas with money for us to take. I will give some freak bitches my tides for you. Amen.''

We both laughed.

We were counting money and drinking for a minute. We had to start our count over from the beginning a couple of times because D-Slug kept saying funny shit that fucked up our count. Everything totaled at $182,000 in cash, and 9½ birds of coke. What made me even happier was the digital scale that was also in Jeff s safe. No more eyeballing, I thought as I looked at it for the hundredth time.

I slid D-Slug $66,000, and I put my exact same share to the side. I put $30,000 in the wall with the lawyer fee, and $20,000 with the flip fee. The work went into shoeboxes with the other coke and I ended up with shoes all over the room.

Now we had 10½ birds of coke, 1¼ birds plus 7¼ ounces of crack, $45,000 in the lawyer fee, and $40,000 in the flip fee. I don't know how much money that D- Slug spent so far but I still had $6,000 in between my mattress. I never even imagined that I would have this much money in my room at one time.

D-Slug spent a few minutes reorganizing his pile of money several times and then looked at me with a look like he was struggling with his inner demons. "Cuz, I'm a keep it funky with you. I need you to hold fitty-five stacks of this for me, so I don't blow it. I wanna cop a spot out by where you gettin one at too, cuz. You know I run through scrilla, and I ain't even got nowhere to put it. I need you to keep me right, JD," D-Slug said with all sincerely.

"I got you, D. Listen, I'm takin Kia to get her ride and find a spot-on Saturday, but I'm goin out there tomorrow. After I take her to pick up her car, I'm a meet you and you can roll back out with us to look for a spot too. I'll talk Kia into putting both cribs in her name, cuz," I said while D-Slug was counting out $55,000 for me to stash.

D-Slug slid the money back to me on the bed and said, "Cuz, I'll be able to manage it in a minute, once I get used to it. Feel me?"

That's when I knew that D-Slug was ready just as much as I was to be The Burgh's next top nigga.

I looked at the seriousness in his eyes. "I feel you, D."

I put D-Slug's money in between the mattress at the top of the bed and put $60,000 of my money in between the mattress at the bottom of the bed with the $6,000 that was already there. I looked at all the money one more time, then lowered the top mattress and looked at D-Slug.

"You know we got one more lick, right?" I asked, already plotting on our next robbery.

D looked surprised. "For what?"

I picked up my $6,000 that was still sitting on top of the bed and began to flip through the bills.

"I was thinkin right, we got enough to sit on, but if all we doin is slangin zips to the niggas, we gonna be sittin on these birds for a minute. With Jeff gone, everybody's gonna be coppin off Tim. But if we get Tim for what he's worth, and slump him, niggas gotta Find new connects," I said and looked under the bed. I continued, "That's when we holla at the niggas, we know was coppin whole thangs and then it's smackin. Feel me, cuz?'

D-Slug nodded his head. "I dig. It's whatever. I know you got it planned out and if it gets us eatin even more, I'll slump whoever," he responded.

"We gonna have to find us a big connect after that though. I'm a probably holla at my dad's people down Virginia," I said, referring to my dad's brother, Uncle Craig.

Uncle Craig is the only person on my dad's side of the family who ever tries to reach out to me. He asked me before if I wanted to move down Norfolk, VA with him and get on his squad. Being that I haven't spoken to my dad in many years, and don't plan on it either, I didn't want to be around anybody that he still associates with. I know I passed up a lot of money, but I rather build from the basement anyway so that nobody can say that they made me. Feel me? Some people might say that I'm stupid for not riding with Uncle Craig, being that he been fucking with heavy birds since the 90's.

"I looked up at the ceiling as I continued, "You know 1 played Uncle Craig, but he'll forgive me when we talk numbers though."

I walked to the closet and pulled out a bottle of Henny while D sat there in a zone.

"Got my mind right and the Chopper held tight/Nigga let me know wutz smackin 2night.

"Who's this?" I asked into the phone, not recognizing the number on the Caller ID.

"It's Boo, nigga. I'm ready. What's up?" Boo asked, tweakin to re-up.

"I'm on my way to the block right now," I replied and hung up.

"Who was that, cuz?" D-Slug asked.

"Boo. That nigga is a fuckin born hustla. This that nigga's second flip, and he started a lawyer fee stash off top. He's ready for that eighthy, cuz."

"Yeah, Boo's on his fuckin grind," D-Slug said as we both stood up and headed out of my bedroom door.

"Is you trying to grab up Laneisha and Mia in a second though?" I asked D.

D-Slug grinned. "Nigga, I was just bout to ask you that same shit."

We drove around the corner to the block, where Boo was standing in front of the cut crib by himself. As soon as he saw me, and D-Slug pull up he began throwing a few jabs and hooks in the air like he was getting ready for the World Championship bout.

"I see you goin hard, cuz," D-slug said to Boo as we got out of the car.

"Yeah, nigga, I'm tryin to cop me a ride next. Fuck that jitney shit, and I definitely ain't catchin the bus. Nothin flashy though, cause I'm tryin to still be chewin," Boo replied and tapped me on the shoulder. "What's up with the re-up though?"

"I got you, cuz," I said, then ran up the steps to the cut crib and into the house.

Gizzle was in the living room with some young ass freak, hugged up on the couch, smoking a blunt. I gave him a head nod and kept it moving before I ended up trying to smash the little broad. I made sure that nobody else was in the crib then crept down into the basement to grab up the 16¼ zips. I then took the work to the dining room and weighed up 4½ zips of crack on my new scale. I put that into a baggie and took the remaining 11¾ zips back downstairs into the stash.

I walked back through the living room so that I could go get Boo. I had to pause for a second because

Gizzle now had the young freak bent over the couch, pounding her from the back. To top it off, ol girl was asshole naked. She looked back at me and licked her lips. Everything inside of me told me to smash her too, but I could not get past the fact that I had a feeling that she was young as fuck and her premature frame gave that belief weight. So, I slowly walked out of the crib.

"Yo, that nigga, Gizzle got this lil ass girl in there takin it from the back with nothing on but sweat." I said to Boo and D-Slug.

D-Slug's eyes lit up. "What you mean by lil ass girl?" D asked already knowing that Gizzle still be knocking off those 12-year old's and shit.

"Cuz, I mean lil ass girl. I mean no titties young." I replied.

"Come on, D, you know Gizzle's bitches be at the bottom of his age group." Boo said and laughed.

I laughed too, but D-Slug had that look in his eyes.

"Shit, if she's fuckin then she's all in. And if she's all in, she's old enough for me," D-Slug said and quickly ran into the crib.

I looked at Boo. "D is a nasty mufucka," I said and we both laughed. "I got that work in there ready for you though."

"That's what I'm lookin for."

We walked into the crib and saw that D-Slug didn't waste any time getting into the action. D was standing on the couch with his dick in the young freak's mouth while Gizzle continued to pound her from behind. She was slurping loud as fuck and looking like a pro. Boo kept walking like he didn't see shit, but I stopped for a couple seconds while the yin and the yang went to war. My dick got hard and as soon as I took one step towards the couch, J-Meanmug came to life on my hip. I looked at the caller ID and saw Laneisa's number. I let it go to my voice mail, but it snapped me out of a lustful zone that would lead to me taking an unnecessary penitentiary chance.

I walked into the dining room. Boo was already sitting in front of the work. He looked at me and shook his head.

"That was quick," Boo joked.

"Naw, cuz, I ain't getting down with that case. I was definitely tempted though."

I admitted. "That's you right there," I said and took the scale off the table and put it in the closet under the bags of junk.

"Yo, JD, I'm trying to be where ya'll niggas is at. Fuck coppin off ya'll, I'm tryin to be coppin with ya'll," Boo said and begun countin $3,600.

"You'll be there sooner than you think the way you flippin," I responded.

D-Slug walked in the room just as Boo handed me the money. Me and Boo both just shook our heads at him.

"I'm sayin though, she got some good ass head, cuz," D-Slug said in defense and then changed the subject. "I see you getting that scrilla, Boo."

Boo put his work inside of his bookbag and stood up. "Yeah, I gotta get back to the money right now though before I miss a dolla."

"Aight, cuz. Holla when you need more." I said as Boo walked through the dining room door. I looked at D-Slug and was going to grind him up for getting some head from that little ass girl, but I decided to keep that all of the way quiet until death.

"We got to get us our own cut crib cause we can't keep all that work down here and definitely not at my mom's crib for too long."

D-Slug had a look of relief. "You right, cuz. And I can tell by the way you talkin you already got something in mind."

"A couple of the apartments in the building on the Ave. is open." I said and hesitated before I finished saying the rest of my plan. "I'm thinkin bout getting one for Laneisha and use that as the cut crib."

D-Slug smiled as if he picked up on the inner-plan. "It sounds good, but you think she'll be with sleepin with birds?"

"I'm positive. She won't say nothing bout it as long as I'm sleepin with her too a couple days a week," I said and laughed.

"I dig it, cuz," D-Slug said and gave me the "Nigga Please" look. "When is we getting ol boy though?"

"Probably Monday or Tuesday. I still got to put the shit together all the way. You know he's that nigga, so we gotta be prepared for it all. Feel me?" I asked to make sure that we were both on the same page.

We began walking through the hallway. I was low-key tweakin to see if girly was still in the living room getting her back banged out.

"Yeah, I feel you. No doubt. I'm leavin whoever stinkin anyway," D-slug replied as we walked into the living room.

Gizzle was playing 007 and the young freak was laying across the couch in just her small bra and a thong, that looked to be at least 3 sizes too big for her small frame. She looked up at me and D and smiled.

"What's your name?" The young freak asked.

"Mike." I lied.

"Did D-Slug tell you how good my head game is?" She asked and seductively put her finger in her mouth.

This little broad is all in already, I thought. My dick instantly got hard as a brick and I knew that my escape was either now or never. "Naw, I'm cool though." I responded and quickly walked out of the front door.

"Don't forget to hit me up tomorrow afternoon." D-Slug said to her before he followed me out of the house.

I looked at him with the look that he was expecting. When I turned back around and began walking down the porch steps D-Slug pointed at a red Regal that was driving down the street towards us.

"That's the ride that came through bustin earlier. I know that ain't bitch ass Walnut," D-slug said and immediately reached for his waist.

Walnut was one of Spade's punk ass flunkies. That nigga never busted a gun in his life, but I guess he wanted to show his loyalty for his dead homie—by becoming somebody else's dead homie.

"Yeah, that's Walnut's shit, cuz. What you tryin ...."

Before I could even finish my sentence D-Slug was dumpin at Walnut with Jeff Rose's Desert Eagle. The sound of the 1st shot reminded me that I had took my Glock out of my closet and put it on my hip when I had put the Henny back before we left my mom's crib. I quickly grabbed my Glock and let the whole clip loose.

The Regal began swerving as he drove past us as fast as possible. The back window disappeared. Me and D-Slug stood there for a second with our guns locked back. It looked as if we both were lusting the gunplay like it was fulfilling a craving or some shit.

We were waiting to see if we hit Walnut and we didn't have to wait long. The Regal drifted on to the sidewalk and then into Mrs. Johnson's porch. There was no movement inside of the car, so Walnut was either dead or very good at playing possum.

We hopped in D's car and smashed off, hoping that nobody saw us. The good thing about Hale Street is that there are only a few livable houses on our street, and most of the people that live in them are women who be at work all day and fiends in the abandoned cribs too high to look out of the window.

D-Slug already knew where to drive us to without me saying anything. We were arguing about whose bullets slumped ol boy and laughing about it, all the way to the Highlevel Bridge in the Homestead section. Once we were driving on the bridge, I took both of our guns and threw them out of the window and over the bridge, kissing the case away.

We shot back to the hood and stopped past Butch's crib to give him the money that I owed him, and then dipped to the Ave.

We pulled up on The Ave. and Laneisha and Mia were standing there waiting like they knew that we were on our way to pick them up. Laneisha had on royal blue stretch-pants shorts and a blue bandanna type of shirt. The shirt was a bandanna folded into a triangle that pointed down to her bellybutton and was tied around her with blue leather straps. Mia had on the same exact outfit, but hers was red (I guess she didn't get the memo). They both was standing there looking sexier than ever.

Laneisha even got her hair done today just for me to fuck it up. I thought as they got into the car.

CHAPTER 12

After a long, lustful night at the Telly, we all went to Scotty's Diner and then me and D-Slug dropped Laneisha and Mia off on The Ave. Once they got out and I closed the door I remembered the plan that I had and called Laneisha back to the car.

"Oh yeah. Neisha Boo make some calls this morning and see if they are renting out one of those apartments in the building on the corner. If they are, get fiend Butch and tell him I said get it. Pay him whatever he wants to handle that." I said as I pulled out some money and counted out $5,500 in all hundred-dollar bills. "I got something to handle. So, I need you to take care of this for me. Aight?" I asked and stuck my hand out of the window with the money in it.

Mia's eyes got big and she was speechless, but Laneisha acted like I only asked her to get me something to drink and was handing her my cup.

"Yeah, Jakill, I got you." Laneisha replied and put the money inside of her purse. "Are you trying to be close to me?" She asked and giggled.

"Closer than you think, sexy. This is for us. I'm coppin us a spot together if that's cool with you."

"You know that's cool with me, Jakill," she said then quickly leaned her head in the window and gave me a long passionate kiss.

When Laneisha pulled her head back out of the window I continued, "Tell Butch to offer them a couple hunnit extra if they can speed us through the process and get the spot today. If we get it, cop a lil bit of furniture and have them deliver it."

She was still smiling ear to ear. "I can't believe that you're doing this, Jakill. I'll have something special for you tonight." Laneisha said.

"Can't baby. I'm goin out of town till Monday. That's why I need you to take care of this for us. But can I get something special when I get back?" I asked and reached out and put my hand on her small bubble.

Instead of Laneisha taking my hand off her ass like I thought that she would, she placed her hand on top of my hand and made me squeeze it.

"Baby, you can get something special anytime that you want it," she replied seductively.

D-Slug cleared his throat. "Can y'all please stop now? My ears are hurtin," he joked.

Mia sucked her teeth.

"I'm a holla at you when I get back cause I'm a be busy makin moves all weekend. Aight?" I asked, hoping that my cover worked.

"As long as you're thinking about me the whole time." Laneisha replied then leaned back into the window and gave me a quick peck on my cheek.

Mia was standing there looking at D-Slug like she expected an apartment or something too.

D-Slug peeped it and couldn't just ignore her, so he said, "Mia, I'm a have something for you too in a minute." Then he pushed the pedal all the way down to the floor and we smashed off.

D-Slug reached to turn on the sounds but stopped. "Damn, cuz. You put me on the spot and shit. Now I got to buy Mia a shoe to live in." D-slug said and we both busted out laughing.

He dropped me off at my mom's crib. Before he pulled off, I told him that I would call him in the morning and tell him where to meet me on Saturday since I can't let Laneisha see me in the hood. And I told him to handle all of the work.

I ran into the crib and straight into my room. My mom was at work, so I was cool. I took the $3,600 from Boo and put it on the ledge in the wall with the flip fee. I grabbed $50,000 from my personal stash under my mattress and laid it on the bed. I walked to the radio and turned on the TI CD and turned the song *"Be Easy"* damn near all the way up. Then I went to my closet and picked out a cream Nike short set to put on and laid it next to the money.

I ran downstairs and took a quick shower while thinking about the money on my bed. Just a couple of weeks ago I was living lick to lick, never thinking that I would be about to grab a spot to live at with my woman, have a hard ass car, and have $50,000 just waiting for me to blow it. Some niggas be in the game for many years and never get to see 50 stacks at one time and here I am just some young jailbird who never had a run on the streets, and I got it like it ain't shit. I can't wait until all my niggas is straight too, I thought as some soap got in my eye and snapped me out of my zone.

I dried off and went back in my room. I turned on the TI song that he be coming at his own neck. This nigga is going to be one of the best because a lot of niggas can't make a song like this, I thought as I put on the short set. I threw on some jewels that I already had on the day before. Then I went into my closet, grabbed a duffle bag and filled it with outfits and shoes that I ain't wear yet. I put the $50,000 in the bag too then put on my white Air Force 1's (low tops) with the cream Nike check and headed out of the door.

I stopped to get a bottle of 151 at the liquor store and then drove to I.U.P.

I pulled up in the parking lot for Kia's dorm and drove slowly through it towards the front door where I saw a group of people standing. I had the T-tops on, the tinted windows up, and the sounds banging that old Michelle song, *"Something In My Heart."* Yeah, I had my swag turned all the way up. Plus, I felt the alcohol buzz kick in, so I felt groovy as fuck.

As I got closer to the group, I recognized Kia and her dormmate there. They were all staring at my car trying to figure out who was behind the wheel and hoping that they had a chance to holla at whoever it was. Kia started smiling from ear to ear. I guess she remembered that I said that I had copped an Iroc Z and just put 2 and 2 together, because as I got a 2-car distance away from her she began walking to my car in slow motion with her sexy ass model walk. When she got to the side of my car, she put her thumb in the air like she was trying to hitchhike. I cracked the tints and motioned for her to get in.

Kia got in the passenger side and crossed her legs, which made her red and white tennis skirt rise to where it couldn't rise anymore, and her entire thighs were out. I glimpsed down with skill, playing it off when I pressed mute so that we could talk and be able to hear each other, at least a little bit. I got ready to say some fly shit but before I could get a word out, she leaned over and gave me the longest kiss in the history of kissing. When our lips separated, we both just happened to look at her friends to see if they were watching. The look on all her friend's faces said it all.

"Damn, daddy, this car is crazy, and you got my friends jealous." Kia said and put her hand on my arm.

"Naw, ya looks got ya friends all jealous," I replied.

I found a parking spot and we sat there for a few minutes listening to the sounds and stuntin on anybody in stuntin reach. Then we walked into the dorm and to Kia's dorm room. Her dormmate must have got the hint because she was nowhere in sight. A couple of broads were peeking out of their doors and around corners to get a good look at me, hoping that I would let them stunt with me one day, as me and Kia walked in and closed the door behind us.

It was lights, cameras, action once that door closed. We both couldn't wait until we got in the room so that we could become one again. Our lips were like magnets as we begun kissing heavily. Our hands were rubbing and caressing all over each other's bodies. My hands quickly found their way under Kia's skirt and her hands found their way down my pants.

Kia broke our kiss. "I'm yours, daddy. Do what you want to me. I know you won't hurt me." She whispered in my ear while her hands

how loud the smacking sound was from me eating her pussy.

I don't know if it was the 151 or my love for her, but I licked from her clit to her ass, ass to her clit, over and over again. That had her going crazy. I kept 2 fingers in her pussy the entire time that I was eating her pussy.

Kia started pulling on my ears, screaming, "I Love you, daddy! I love you, daddy! I love you, daddy! I'm cumming!"

I kissed my way back up her stomach and sucked on her titties while still fingering her for a few minutes, letting her cum down my hand. Then I picked her up and carried her over to the wooden desk and sat her on top of it. I began kissing her passionately and we were both breathing heavy from the lust and love. I rubbed my hands down her body to her ankles and then held her legs up in the air spread wide apart. I looked down and saw Kia's dripping wet pussy just staring at me. My dick was extremely hard and standing straight out. It was positioned perfectly in line with her pussy, so I leaned in a little bit and made my dick rub on her clit.

"Put it in, baby," I said thinking about how long it took me to get inside of her tight pussy the last time.

Kia hesitated, but still put it in and tensed from the initial pain until it got comfortable to her.

"Oh, Kia. Damn, girl, this pussy's good as fuck! Yeah, baby, take this dick!" I said as I thrust in and out of her faster and harder with each stroke.

"I'm taking it, daddy," she moaned in between deep

breaths and went back to screaming again.

"I'm bout to nut, baby." I said and immediately busted all up in her.

After a few extra short strokes, I said to her, "Baby, I would love to go forever but we gotta get up early in the morning cause I got a surprise for you."

After about 2 hours of screaming and semen we went to sleep.

We woke up at 7:00 AM still exhausted. I had to use the men's shower on the men's floor because some hating ass broads was protesting me getting in their shower with Kia.

After a quick shower and the regular, me and Kia was in my ride on the way to The Burgh with Dru Hill muted.

"What's so special, daddy?" Kia asked curiously.

"You gotta see it to believe it, baby. It's a couple things that's gonna take up the whole day," I replied.

Kia seductively licked her lip and leaned over the gear shifter. "I have something special for you too later." She said in her sexy voice.

"Oh yeah? What's that?"

"I want you to show me how to give you head so I

can bless you like you bless me, daddy."

I almost crashed into a guardrail going around a bend. I controlled the car and just nodded my head at Kia, thinking about how similar her and Laneisha are but so different. After a long pause, I turned the sounds up and I drove while Kia dozed off.

I woke Kia up as we pulled into the car lot. She blinked a few times to make sure that her vision was focusing right and then looked at me confused.

"Are you about to buy another car?" She asked.

"I already bought another car." I said and watched Dave point to a black Benz with the top down, showing off the peanut butter leather interior, and it had a red ribbon tied around it in a bow.

Kia didn't peep Dave's gesture. "For what?" She asked.

I put my arm around her waist and turned her in the direction of the Benz. "For who?" I replied and guided her to the car. "A king can't be fly if his queen ain't. Dig me?"

Kia looked at the car and then at me. "Baby, you bought me a brand-new fucking Benz?" She asked excitedly.

"I said I had something special for you."

Kia jumped up and down in excitement while I watched her big titties bounce too.

Dave crept up on us and told Kia to "sit in the driver seat and see if it feels new."

Kia gave me a long hug and a million kisses before she climbed into her new car and allowed me and Dave to walk away to conduct business in his office.

Once we got inside of Dave's office, he closed the door and the blinds, which made me feel a little uncomfortable since I been paranoid for the past week. He sat behind his desk and then I sat down after I was sure that this wasn't any type of set-up.

Dave cut straight through the bullshit. "Look, buddy, this is how it works. You pay for it now and I'm going to give you post-dated receipts for the next thirty-six months. That way it looks like she bought it in payments. Follow me?"

"Yeah, I'm with you, but you sure there's no way it'll bounce back on my girl?" I asked a little skeptical of Dave's plan.

Dave chuckled. "Everything's official. I already did the receipts. I just have to put your lady friend's info on them, and she has to fill out the rest of the paperwork. Oh, and I called the insurance agent, John, when I saw you pull up. He's on his way over right now. Do you want to get insurance on the other two cars as well? Because I know your uncle's insurance card was bogus," Dave said and chuckled again.

After a half hour long paperwork session, Kia owned a brand-new Benz CLK320 with legitimate insurance. I gave her a few slow jam CDs and told her to follow me to George Aiken's restaurant Downtown.

Kia immediately put on Mary's CD and turned the loud factory sounds up before we pulled off. I turned on the 1st Silkk *The Shocker* CD and let the song, *"Mr."* drown out her sounds and anybody else's who was within a mile.

When we were halfway to Downtown, I turned down the sounds and called D-Slug. "What's smackin, cuz?" I asked into my earpiece.

"Ain't shit, JD," D-Slug responded and then got right down to business. "TK, Tre. May four. Wokky, deuce. Hurt, two and three quarters. Boo, Daz, and Gizzle still rockin for the time being."

"Niggas is getting it, huh?"

"Yeah. The cut is dry now and I don't want to go up

in Auntie's crib and get cussed out for leavin with a bag full of who-knows-what. Feel me?" D-Slug said, confirming that all the work at the cut crib was gone.

I smiled at the thought of more money being made by doing nothing. "Fuck it, D. Niggas can wait till later. Meet me at George Aikens Downtown ASAP. We bout to go look for some spots. How much money you got on you?"

"I still got like nine stacks and some change, plus ten- two for the flip."

I had to slow down a little bit because I saw a State Trooper's car ducked off in a homemade cut off to the side of the parkway. There's no way that he would be able to catch me, but I don't want to get my Iroc hot already.

"Aight, look. Keep five of the flip for right now in case you find something, you'll have more than enough to get what you need for it. I'll just grab it out ya stash and put it back. Give me the fitty-two so I can balloon my pockets a lil bit more. Oh, yeah, I just grabbed Kia that Benz," I said and waited for a joke that I knew was coming.

"Hell no, cuz! I thought you were jus bullshittin. How much it run you?" He asked, holding back on the joke.

"Thirty-five."

"What, you gonna grab Laneisha a Benz too?" D-Slug joked and began laughing.

"Naw. I was thinkin bout a Lex." I quickly shot back and laughed too even though I was dead serious. I had already thought about buying a Lexus for Laneisha and like they say, "It ain't trickin if you got it and I got it."

D-Slug made it to George Aiken's 5 minutes after me and Kia got there. Kia's Benz was parked directly in front of the entrance with the ribbon still tied around it, making everybody who walked past it stop and admire for a few minutes including D-Slug.

D walked in the restaurant and right over to our table. He looked at me and then at Kia and shook his head with a smirk on his face.

"What is you doin to my cuz, Kia?" D asked jokingly.

Kia looked at me and smiled. "What is your cousin doing to me?" She said and gave me a quick kiss. She then looked back at D-Slug. "What are you doing here anyway, D?"

D-Slug sat down at the table with us and turned his

Duke Blue Devils fitted hat to the back. "I'm bout to cop a spot out there too." He said, assuming I had already told Kia about getting us a crib.

I turned to Kia, who was about to say something until I cut her off. "Oh, baby, I almost forgot to tell you what the other surprise is." I said and then paused for a second to let the suspense get to her then continued, "I'm coppin me and you a spot out by ya school."

Kia's eyes lit up. "For real, baby? You doing all of this for me? I love you, daddy," she said excitedly enough for everybody in the restaurant to turn towards us expecting to see me down on one knee or some shit.

"We gonna look around and see what we can find for us and a spot for D." I said as Kia put her hand under the table low key and slid it up my shorts and played with the tip of my dick for a couple seconds.

We spent the next half hour eating Buffalo Wings and macaroni and cheese. We were all tweakin for our next event that it looked like we were forcing ourselves to eat the food. Then we were on the road on our way out to Indiana County.

Us 3 were shitting on everybody else that was driving. People were almost crashing just to get a look at our cars. I swear it looked like some movie shit. A Benz with a bow on it, followed by a white and royal blue bowling ball Iroc Z, and that was followed by a royal blue Mustang sitting on Chrome D's. Somebody in an old school Cutlass was staring so hard that he had almost missed his exit and had to hit sideways in order to turn off on the off ramp.

For most of the drive I was banging that Makevelli CD and the song, *"Hail Mary"* was making me get back on that paranoid shit again. *Niggas can probably assume that me and D-slug are behind these licks and bodies, but even if there were witnesses they wouldn't know who we were because the only motherfucker that we had ever robbed without masks on was Tizz's bitch ass on my birthday and that little piece of shit that we had got off of him wasn't worth me being paranoid about.* I thought.

I reached over and got the left over 151 and drank the paranoidness away while the song *"Crazy"* made me think about how it's going to be when my brother gets out.

After looking at only 3 houses, all about 1 mile away from the campus. Kia chose a tan colored 3-bedroom house with a 2-car garage for rent. It even had a front yard with a flower-lined walkway that led to the side entrance to the basement. I decided on turning most of the basement into my game room with all types of shit in it, especially a pool table and eventually an in-house theater. I had to laugh to myself at the thought of that *stuntastic shit.* I tossed our new landlord a couple extra hundred dollars on top of the security deposit and 1st month's rent. The landlord liked the extra gift and told us that we could move in today.

D-Slug said that a house was too big for him right now, so he only wanted to get an apartment. He's really trying to learn how to manage his money better. I thought while Kia was taking care of the paperwork for D's 2-bedroom apartment 3 blocks away from me and Kia's spot. D tossed his landlord some extra cash, but the landlord told him that he couldn't move in until Wednesday.

The 3 of us spent the rest of the day furniture shopping and all that good shit that I realized was boring as fuck if you have a woman picking out most of the shit.

D-Slug then went back to The Burg and me and Kia went to our new crib. To break in our new house, she broke down and gave me some head. *You could tell that this was her 1st time because it wasn't really about shit, but she'll learn.* I thought as Kia's teeth got me again.

CHAPTER 13

Sunday afternoon I told Kia that I had to stay in The Burgh for a couple of days so that I can keep the money right. She didn't get mad or anything. I love this girl, I thought while I was headed to my mom's crib.

I lucked up and made it there before my mom got back from church. I knew that I didn't have a lot of time before my mom came home on some "the Lord told me to have a talk with you" shit. So, I rushed to my room and put the flip fee back from me and D-Slug's stash. Then I grabbed the byrd of crack out of a shoe box and put it in a duffle bag. I grabbed a bottle of vodka out of the closet and left back out of the crib in route to the cut crib.

It looked like an angry mob on the block as I pulled up and seen niggas lined up waiting to re-up. I realized that it was fucked up of me to leave the niggas without work like that.

"Cuz, we been down here all morning trying to flip," Daz said as soon as I stepped out of the car.

"I know you came prepared," Boo said while

looking at my duffle bag.

I patted the bag. "Let me know what y'all niggas need and I'm a go in the spot and holla back in a couple minutes.

Boo wanted another 4½. Daz and Teeke wanted 3½. Mayo wanted 4½. Gizzle and Hurt both wanted 3. E- Wok wanted 2 again. We can see who the hustlers are.

After I served all the niggas, they ran back to getting that money and I put the left-over 12 zips in the stash once the crib was clear. I put the scale back in the closet and put the $19,200 in my bag then dipped out of the spot.

I got in my car and took a few gulps of vodka while I watched the niggas serve clucks up and down The Tre. I was about to start my car up when I saw the Task Force turn on our block in back to back Tauruses. I ducked behind the tints, thinking that they might have saw me, until they kept going. Once they were out of sight, I started up my car and peeled off while niggas were all coming back out of the bushes and alleys. I kept the sounds off just in case the Task Force was somewhere lurking.

I thought about the rest of the coke, so I called Butch. "Yo, how many eggs can you scramble at once?" I asked hoping that he would catch on to the code.

"However, many you put in the skillet, lil nigga. I keep tellin you I still got it," Butch shot back like he had to protect his chef skills.

"I'll see you in a minute," I said and hung up on him before he could start his stories.

I drove around to The Ave. and pulled up behind D-Slug's 5.0, which D and Mia were hugged up leaning against. They both walked to my car, holding hands and smiling. I grabbed my CD case and sped through it, trying to find my Master P Ghetto Dope CD so I could blast the song, "Captain Kirk", but I couldn't get it before they were both leaning through the window so I aborted my joke.

"Guess where ya Neisha Boo's at," Mia said, still smiling.

I was already wondering that because I know that she's off work on the weekends. "Where she at?" I asked to entertain Mia's Q and A.

"She's at y'all love nest," D-slug said and laughed.

I can't believe that I had forgot about Laneisha getting us an apartment. I also can't believe that she had made it happen. She continues to impress me, I thought and caught myself smiling.

"Is one of y'all love birds," I dragged out love birds

so that it had that much more emphasis and continued, "gonna let me know which spot I live in?"

"Five-D" D-Slug snapped back a little bit mad.

"I'll holla at y'all love birds a lil bit later," I said and peeled off without letting D-Slug respond.

I had to drive all the way around the corner because the building is on the corner before you get to the row houses. I parked on the side where the park is and walked to the front of the brown building. The entrance door always be unlocked because kids always be running in and out of it.

A few of the hood bitches stay in the building, so I'm going to have to be low key and keep a burner pointed at the door just in case one of their hook-ups get a stupid idea. I doubt anybody try me though, I thought and then checked myself for thinking like everybody that me and D robbed.

I walked up the door. Laneisha opened the door before I even knock. Mia must have called her to let her know that I was on my way.

She was standing prissy steps and down the short, dirty, hallway to our there looking sexy as fuck in just some tight stretch shorts and a black bra. Her hair was down, hanging way past her shoulders without the weave in it.

Laneisha instantly jumped on me and wrapped her legs around me. "Welcome home, Jakill," she said and kissed me.

Once our lips separated, I carried her through all of the rooms and couldn't believe that she had the whole spot done up already. Our bedroom had a king size bed, 2 small dressers and a large one, a nightstand with a lamp on both sides of the bed, a long mirror mounted to the back of the bedroom door, a 30-something inch TV, and the sounds that I had bought her.

The guestroom was basic with a queen size bed, one dresser, one nightstand and a 19-inch TV.

The living room, however, had a 3-piece black leather couch hook-up, an all glass coffee table with the 2 matching side tables—they even had magazines on them already—and a 60-inch big screen TV.

Our apartment didn't have a dining room, but the kitchen had enough room and a table in it that sat 6.

"I can't believe you got the spot laid out that quick with on fitty-five hunnits." I said as I ushered her back into the living room. Laneisha smiled.

"Come on, baby, I make it happen. I even went grocery shopping. I had to use twenty-five hundred that I had saved up too." She replied.

"I'm a give you that back."

"No, I'm good. I had to pitch in somehow. You always lace me anyway," she said and looked at me confused. "I thought you wasn't coming back until Monday."

"I wasn't, but I missed you too much." I smoothly replied.

Laneisha put her arms around my neck. "Is that right, Jakill?" She said and then kissed me.

My dick instantly got hard, but I had money on my mind. "Baby, before we fully break the crib in. I got to make some runs and shit, but I got something to hold you off."

"What's that?" She asked seductively.

I laid her down on the loveseat and kneeled in front of her. She closed her eyes and tweaked for my tongue as I pulled her shorts to the side, exposing her wet, recently trimmed, pussy. Her thong was between her pussy lips until I pulled that to the side as well. I put my face between her legs and ate her pussy at the fastest pace that I could until she came.

"Your set of keys are on the hook to your left," she said as I was about to walk out of the door.

I grabbed the keys off of the wooden hook on the wall to the left of me and smiled when I saw that they were on a Chevrolet keychain.

"I love you, Neisha Boo." I said honestly.

"You always did, and I always loved you," she said before I closed the door.

I got in my car and drove straight to my mom's crib. I went in the house and put the $19,200 from the niggas in the flip stash. Then I grabbed 614 birds still in shoe boxes and bounced right back out of the crib before my mom got back.

I drove around to Butch's spot, so I could get this shit cooked up. As usual I was on auto pilot as I drove and thought about money. I pulled up to his crib.

Butch's front door was wide open and when I got out of the car, I could see him standing in the doorway dancing. I walked up the porch steps as he walked out onto the porch.

"Butch, what's smackin?" I asked over Al Green.

I couldn't help but to laugh at this smoker's routine.

"I been dancing in my apron for a while, lil nigga. How much we cheffin up?" Butch asked and did something that resembled Dion Sanders' touchdown celebration.

"Six and a half whole thangs."

Butch's eyes got bigger than usual. He grabbed my shoulder. "Damn, lil nigga. you just blew up overnight."

That comment made me wonder who else thought that same thing.

We went inside of his crib. I sat on the crate and gulped Thunderbird and talked on my phone while Butch did what he did.

When Butch was done cooking, I gave him $3,200 and bounced back to my mom's crib without running into the Task Force.

I wasn't as lucky when I walked in my mom's front door.

"The Lord told me that it's time for us to have a talk." My mom said and scared the shit out of me because she was hiding behind the door.

I'm glad that I left my gun in the car. I thought.

"Yeah, but a I'm a holla at you when I get done moving." I said and began running up the steps.

"Where are you moving to?" She asked clearly in shock or was just a good actress.

I acted like I didn't hear her as I ran up the 3rd floor steps and into my room. I put all the work inside of a garbage bag. I counted how much money was in each stash, wrote it down, and then put all the money inside of the bag as well. Then I put all my brand-new outfits and shoes inside of the bag too.

My mom didn't try to say anything else to me as I carried my bag out of her house. She just stood there with a look on her face like she wish she could have said what she wanted to say.

I put the bag on the back seat and smashed off. I left the sounds turned off due to the fact I had 10½ birds and almost $ 180,000 on the back seat, and a dirty Chopper in the trunk.

I was a half of block away from my new crib when I heard sirens and saw the flashing lights on a black Ford Taurus speeding up behind me. My mind immediately started racing trying to figure out what I was about to do. Just as I was about to open the engine on them the Taurus turned left at the intersection that I had just passed. I lit up a lit up a Newport to calm my nerves. I looked in the rearview to make sure that they didn't turn around. Then I wiped away the sweat that formed on my forehead that quick.

I pulled up on the side of the building and parked in the same spot as last time. *This is my new parking spot.* I thought as I got out of the car. I leaned back in the car and put my phone's SIM card on top of the sunvisor. Then I got the bag from the back seat and headed to our apartment looking like I'm just finishing moving in.

Dirty Mike was walking out of the building as I was walking in.

"What's smackin, cuz?" I spoke.

"Nothin," dirty Mike replied in his usual miserable state.

He probably was hating on me for carrying a black garbage bag instead of a LV luggage bag or some shit. If he only knew how much this Hefty is really worth? I thought as I kept walking up the steps.

I walked in the crib and went straight to the guestroom. Laneisha was in our bedroom, but quickly ended up standing in the guestroom doorway.

"Listen, baby, I'm gonna have shit in the guestroom closet till we get a safe, so make sure nobody goes in there.

Aight?" I asked referring to Mia but used a tone that wouldn't make her feel like I'm giving her orders.

"Mia ain't going to be anywhere in this room, Jakill." She said to let me know that she knew who I was referring to. Then she sat down on the bed. "Do you need any help stashing it?"

"Naw, I'm cool, baby." I said thinking about how she never ceases to amaze me.

I stacked the coke and crack shoe boxes in the guestroom closet under boxes that had my shoes in them. I put my $10,800 and D-Slug's $50,000 in between the mattress in me and Laneisha's room. I emptied all the Captain Crunch cereal out of the box and into a large Tupperware bowl. Then I put the lawyer fee into the Captain Crunch box and put it in the kitchen cabinet. The flip fee went inside of a small garbage bag and inside of the refrigerator, under the vegetables.

Once I was done stashing shit me and Laneisha took a long shower and I tore her ass up before we went to sleep in our new bed for the first time.

CHAPTER 14

I got up early in the morning and the first thing that I was thinking about was jackin Tim Murphy tonight instead of waiting. *Yeah, we're going to get him tonight. Fuck it!*

Laneisha was up earlier than me cooking us breakfast so that we could eat before it was time for me to drop her off at school. This is the first time a woman that wasn't related cooked me breakfast at the crack of dawn. Don't get me wrong, I had broads cook for me many times, but I'm talking about early in the morning when it's still dark outside. *Kia better do the same shit.* I thought as I ate a fork full of homefries.

After I dropped off Laneisha at school I was out and about in my Iroc, with the sounds off, planning out this lick.

"*Got my mind right and the Chopper held tight/ Nigga let me know wutz smackin 2night.*

I looked at the Caller ID and instantly thought about more money. "What's smackin, Boo?" I answered.

Boo was breathing heavy into the phone. "Cuz." he

said and paused to catch his breath before he continued, "Don't come round the block. It's hot as fuck. Where can I meet you at?"

I immediately assumed that the *Task Force grabbed up some of the niggas. At least we can afford to get the homies lawyers.* I thought. "Meet me at One-Stop in five minutes. What's up, cuz?"

"I'll holla in five." He said and hung up.

I called D-Slug.

"What?" D-Slug asked clearly still sleep. "D, what's smackin?" I asked into my earpiece.

"Cuz, do you know what time it is?" D-Slug asked angrily.

"Something went down on the block. I'm bout to pick up Boo and find out what."

"Yeah, it looks like Boo left me a couple voicemails. JD, I'm bout to hit the snooze button, but when you find out what's what, hit me back. Aight?"

"Yeah," I said as I turned the corner by the store. "And tell Mia I love her." I joked and then hung up.

I pulled up at One-Stop and Boo appeared out of the bushes sweating profusely and holding a duffle bag. He quickly got in and put the bag on the back seat. We smashed off in silence.

After a few minutes of driving towards East Liberty I broke the silence. "What the fuck's goin on, cuz?"

Boo looked at me to let me know that he was about to say some serious shit. "E-Wok got slumped." He said in a soft tone that you wouldn't expect when one of your niggas get killed.

I hit the brakes and almost caused the car behind me to crash into my car.

"JD keep going before we get hopped on." Boo said and made sense.

I pulled off. "Who the fuck did it Boo? Ain't nobody from the block getting slumped and I ain't gonna ride for em. That nigga died over me, cuz. Me, cuz." I was snapping.

Boo looked at me again. "Listen, JD I slumped him." Boo said calmly.

That's when I noticed that he wasn't looking me in my eyes but watching my hands. I almost crashed into the car in front of me that stopped to make a left turn.

He continued before I could speak. "I came round the block and seen him tip toein out the spot with this bag here, lookin round like he was checkin to see if anybody was watchin him. You know, on that nervous shit. I crept up on him and asked him what he had in the bag. Wok just started stutterin and shit."

I was still trying to register the fact that one of my niggas killed one of my niggas, even though E-Wok wasn't one of my closest niggas.

Boo kept explaining what happened. "I knew something was wrong, so I tried to reach for the bag and cuz pulled out that lil ass chrome twenty-five. JD, he pulled the trigger, but that dumb mufucka had the safety on. Yo, I grabbed my nine off my hip quick as fuck and lit his ass up before he could even take that safety off." Boo lit up a Newport.

"I grabbed the bag and dipped. Soon as I got a chance, I looked in the bag and called D cause he said you was gonna be gone till tonight or some shit, but when I kept getting his voicemail, I hit you up."

I was still trying to analyze the whole situation.

"So, what's in the bag?" I asked confused.

He grabbed the duffle bag and opened it up. "That snake mufucka tried to get you, cuz."

I looked in and immediately knew that I was staring at the 12 ounces from the cut crib stash. That made this situation easy to deal with.

"That's about twelve zips, cuz. Keep it. You earned that shit, nigga. You showed me how thorough I knew you was. Get money with us." I said and gave him a pound.

We rode around in silence for about a half hour until I turned on the new J-Meanmug CD, which is the soundtrack for his DVD, 40 Foot Wall. I put on his song, *"Bitches & Paper,"* and the catchy sing songy book grabbed me.

"See, I got a lot of bitches and got paper on my mind/ 150 shots squeezing, I'm the reason haters diein/ And I'm stickin to the script, never snitchin is the code/ any beef just grab the heat and load a clip, then let it blow."

I dropped off Boo at his BM's crib and called D-Slug as soon as Boo got out of the car. "Cuz, you won't believe this shit," I said when D-Slug answered the phone.

"What's up?" D-Slug asked waiting to find out what my earlier call was about.

I lit up a Newport and took a long hit. "The nigga, Boo, is official, cuz. Ol boy, Wokky, tried to eat the twelve pies out the spot and cuz peeped game. The nigga sent dude to holla at Spade."

"Damn. So, he flighted him, huh?" D-Slug asked excitedly.

"Hell, yeah, on some thorough shit. And as for the pies, I let him keep em and told him to get money with us, since he showed his loyalty."

D-Slug did his sinister laugh. "I always knew cuz had that thoroughness in him. Real shit, JD. You can see that shit in Boo and look at the way he was tossin em when the rest of the niggas was barely turnin em over. I love that nigga."

"Yeah though, I had the other dude put six and a half cakes in the oven last night. But on another note D, that business is smackin tonight."

"That's what the fuck I'm talkin bout, cuz." D-Slug said loud enough to cause Mia to ask what happened? in the background.

"I'll holla when you come through. I'll be posted up on The Rows."

"I'll be there soon as Mia get done with all this cosmo class shit. She should of went to school today for all that shit," he said before we hung up.

I drove up to The Ave. There were a couple fiends out just bullshitting. All the bitches must have been in school or still sleep. The only nigga out was Drizzy who was walking up the steps to go in Keva's mom's crib.

I been thinking about putting him on too for the past couple of days on the strength of Keva and Pooh. I got out of my car just as he was about to walk inside of the door.

"Yo, Drizzy! Let me holla at you for a minute." I hollered before he walked inside.

He looked back and quickly reached for his burner until he saw that it was me with no gun in my hand.

"Damn, homie, I thought I got caught slippin out this bitch. You know when you hear 'let me holla at you' it makes a nigga think it's on or some shit. What's up though?" Drizzy asked curiously but was still looking around on alert.

"Look, cuz, you aight nigga and I fuck with you. I'm a keep it three hunnit with you. Ya squad is butt. Niggas be broke as fuck and I don't like seein nobody I fuck with scratchin and surviving."

Drizzy's pride and ego spoke. "Hold up, cuz, I ain't starving."

"Naw, I ain't pocket checkin or challenging ya hustle. What I'm saying is, I'm a holla at you tomorrow and set you straight under the same circumstances as my niggas from The Tre," I said and watched Drizzy's facial expression say that he was thinking hard about what I was proposing.

"What's the circumstances though?"

"All you gotta do is let me know if you trying to eat or not and we'll rap about the details tomorrow." I replied.

Drizzy stared at the sky and smiled. "You're a thorough ass nigga, JD, and I respect that. Plus, it wouldn't hurt to be pushin something like that bowlin ball shit you pushin. Nigga, I'll be here all-day tomorrow," he replied eagerly.

Since there wasn't really nobody on The Ave. I didn't want to post up there, so I ended our conversation. "I'm a let you get back to what you were about to do, but I'm a swing through tomorrow morning like ten."

Even though I still want to fuck Keva, the fact is that Drizzy's a cool motherfucker that just can't get over the hump. *I'm going to give him a small push because he got to be able to take better care of his daughter, Pooh,* I thought as I got in my car.

I drove down SQ and got flagged down by one of my young freaks that I just cut off. Since I had some time to waste while I waited for D-Slug I decided to pull over and bullshit with her for a second.

"Yo, Chanel! Hop in." I said once I turned the sounds down.

Chanel is a straight hoodrat but sexy as fuck. Dark skin, 6', about 140-lbs, with big titties, and long ass legs. To top her off, she got big hazel eyes. She's also 2 years older than me. I met her coming out of Dorsey's Record Store last month and got some of that good pussy and great brain 10 minutes later. She's one of them broads that could go to another hood and all the niggas would try to wife her.

"Nigga, you ain't holla at me in over a week and you think you just gonna pick me up and get some pussy. Nigga, you got the wrong bitch." Chanel snapped.

I laughed so hard that she walked away from my car calling me every single name that she could think of. I had no intentions on fucking her. I just wanted to bullshit until D-Slug came through, so I wasn't mad. I'm really trying to just rock out with Kia and Laneisha. I thought and shook my head in disbelief of how my situation was.

I didn't know how hot the block was still and I didn't want to be the one to find out. I ended up driving back up the Ave. since I knew that D-Slug should be coming through in a little bit. I parked and sat on the cement wall on the side of the row crib steps and finished planning out this lick.

About 20 minutes later D-Slug and Mia finally pulled up with the sounds banging that old Smamez Loc song, *"Bad Wayz."* I had just missed the part where Smamez Loc say, *"I'm lookin down on niggas I used to look up/ Mr. Lowkey, y'all niggas, many all talk too much."* That's how I feel now—I'm looking down on niggas that I used to look up to (niggas like Jeff Rose and Tim Murphy).

"What's up?" D-Slug asked as they got out of his car and snapped me out of my zone.

"JD." Mia greeted me.

"What's smackin D and Lil D?" I asked, and Mia giggled.

"You talk to Boo again." D-Slug asked, trying to act like my comment didn't bother him.

"Not since I dropped him off at his BM's."

D-Slug gave Mia a quick sloppy kiss. "Mia, I'm a holla at you later. Let me rap to my cuz for a minute," D-Slug said.

"Aight, baby. I'm bout to see what's up with my sis and niece anyway," Mia responded then looked at me. "JD is Laneisha at y'all love nest?"

"Nope. She's at school, where ya ass need to be." I replied.

Mia sucked her teeth and walked up the steps.

"So, what's the drill?" D-Slug asked once Mia was out of hearing range.

"Yo, I think I was doin too much planning on this one. I was tryin to think of the right way to get him and where to catch him at, but I just realized that he's always protected by niggas when he's out. So, the only way to get him is like how we got Spade's bitch ass. But we gotta catch this nigga comin home when he's most likely by himself."

D really didn't give a fuck when we catch Tim and I knew it.

"Yeah, that would be better." He said and paused, "But if niggas are with him, I'm clappin off top, cuz."

"There's an abandoned crib next door to his spot, so we gonna lay low in that mufucka tonight from eight till the nigga show up."

D-slug looked at his fingers and acted like he was counting something. "So, what if he doesn't show till like three somethin?" He asked.

"Then you better take a shit, by eight." I replied seriously.

D laughed but knew that I was dead serious.

I stood up and began walking to the side of my car. "I'm bout to pick up Laneisha from school. Meet me down here at seven-thirty, cuz. No later. And bring Daz's mom's car with you." I said and got in my car.

"Let's get it." D-Slug said right before I pulled off.

I got to Westinghouse High School before it let out, so I talked to Kia on the phone for a few minutes about all the extra shit she had bought for our crib. I told her that I'll be home tomorrow night and she didn't even trip. That's probably because she's too busy spending my money, I thought. Then dismissed that thought as me just thinking about how these regular hood bitches be. I know that Kia ain't like that.

I ended the call when I saw Laneisha walking to the corner where I was parked at. She got in and we went straight to the crib.

I'm trying to spend a lot of time with her since I'll probably be chillin with Kia until Friday. I got to play my part, even though me and Laneisha never actually said that we were a couple or anything special. There's no contract or a verbal agreement. I still have to show her some respect and give her at least some of my time. This juggling shit is hard when you're in a situation like mine, but it is what it is.

I got 2 good ones when most niggas don't even have one. Kia is just the number one because she is more thorough in a lot of aspects. I thought while me and Laneisha were watching *Friday After Next* on the big screen TV in the living room.

There was a knock at the door.

It was D-Slug standing there out of breath.

I immediately thought that some more crazy shit happened on the block until D-Slug grinned.

"Cuz, they gotta get a mufuckin elevator in this bitch." D-Slug said as he walked in the crib.

"Nigga, how you be running through all them hoes and can't run up these lil bit ass steps?" I asked jokingly.

"That's cause I step on em, not up em," he shot back.

"Yo, I need some cake though. Niggas are butt."

"What niggas need?" I asked as I led D towards the guestroom.

D-Slug took off his bookbag that was strapped over

one shoulder and dumped a pile of money out of it onto the bed. "I just wrote they shit, down, grabbed they cheddar, and told em I'll be back." He said and pulled out a small piece of paper. D looked at the paper and continued, "Daz, six. TK, five and a half. Mayo, seven. Gizz, four and a half. Hurt, four and a half. That's twenty-seven and a half, and twenty-two stacks right there."

I took the piece of paper out of D's hand to make sure that he wasn't just bullshittin. It had all of the shit D had just said written on it.

"Yo, D, niggas are flippin fast as fuck. I gotta work on that connect too then while I'm out Indiana for the rest of the week, and I gotta remember to cop a safe."

"Shit, I don't know why. We keep provin that ain't shit safe about a safe anyway." D-Slug said and laughed.

"I'm definitely not goin out like them niggas though," I said and picked up the money to change subjects.

I put $15,000 in the refrigerator and $7,000 in the cereal box. I showed D-slug where all the stashes were.

"I'm takin the lawyer fee to my other spot so Kia could get us lawyers if we happen to get booked." I said.

D just nodded his head in agreement as he weighed

MORE BIRDS MORE BODIES

up all the niggas' orders and put them in separate bags.

CHAPTER 15

At 7:27 p.m., D-Slug pulled up on The Ave. in Daz's mom's car, smoking some dro.

D cracked the passenger side window. "You ready?" He asked in between puffs.

I didn't respond. I just walked to my car, which was parked directly in front of his, and grabbed my Chopper and bag out of the trunk. Then I got in Daz's mom's car. I reached in my bag and pulled out my Lyfe CD and a pint of vodka.

"I ain't forget this time, nigga." I said and put in the CD as D pulled off still smoking.

"And they teasin me with these 23's and these DVD's in their rides/and they pass me by, by, by, by, by, by and have the nerve to wonder why/I be robbin these niggas"

Lyfe continued to sing as I thought about using some of Tim's money to put TV's and DVD's in my Iroc Z. That's that Homiwood thinking, I guess.

We pulled up a block away from Tim's crib and put

our masks and gloves on.

"I'm feelin like killin every nigga with him tonight. That Sour D got me where I need to be." D said excitedly.

"I'm a lil aight off this bottle, cuz." I said and looked at the bottle of vodka like it was going to vouch for me. "You know I don't give a fuck. Let it do what it do!"

We got out of the car and crept through the cuts all the way to the abandoned crib.

The abandoned crib wasn't like no hood abandoned crib with roaches and rats running around. It was a nice 3 floor house that nobody moved in for a few months or so. It still had some furniture in it, and it smelled like mothballs. The only thing wrong with it was the back door that D-Slug had just kicked completely off the hinges. The good thing is that it had a perfect view of Tim's house.

Tim didn't live anything like Jeff, I thought as I looked out of the window at Tim's regular brown 3 floor crib. It looked like something that your grandmother would live in. One of those real quiet looking cribs. There weren't even any cars in the driveway. Nothing fancy. I guess that's how he kept the Feds off him all this time. That made me think about how much money he's probably stashing.

D-Slug was looking over my shoulder.

"Either that nigga ain't home or he's sleep early cause ain't no lights on at all," he said in a tone like he was tired of waiting already.

"You might as well fall back. We gonna be here a minute. I got the window, D."

I pulled one of the couches over to the window and relaxed. I knew that we were more than likely going to be there for a while. So, I called Laneisha and then Kia for a minute. I spent some time thinking about the 2 of them. Kia had told me that she ran through all the money on shit for the crib, so I knew that I had to bring some change with me up there besides the lawyer fee. I wondered if she was just trying to get out on me for as much money as possible. I had to laugh at that because I know that she was right there before I was getting money like I am now. I might have copped her that Benz too early in our relationship though. That reminded me that I had to cop Laneisha a car too. The crazy thing is that Laneisha probably don't even want one. She's not on that materialistic shit. *Kia is the guaranteed rider though.* I reminded myself.

I didn't want to be on that lovey dovey vibe before this lick. So, I called Boo and the rest of the homies to see how they felt about that E-Wok shit. All the niggas had already known what went down and they understood it. I let them know that I'm rockin with Boo on that shit and the niggas from The Tre had to be that loyal to each other.

All the while my eyes had never left Tim's crib.

D was posted up on the steps in the hallway, probably so I couldn't hear him talking all sweet to Mia. He acts like I can't see that they are deeper than how he act like they are. Once I saw them holding hands on The Ave. I knew what it was hittin for. I thought and laughed. I can't believe that a broad finally locked him down. And it had to be a hood freak. Maybe it's just hard for me to see the right qualities in the wrong people. I was thinking until I saw Tim's "Money Green" SS Monte Carlo driving down the street towards us.

"Yo, D! Come on, cuz, here he come." I said and looked at my watch, seeing that it was a little bit after 2:00 a.m.

Without any more words being said, we both picked up our Choppers, put our masks and gloves back on, then ran out of the back door. D-Slug followed my lead as we ran though Tim's backyard and ran around his crib so that we could creep up on his blind side.

We stopped on the side of his crib and hid in some bushes so that we could wait and see who was in the car with him.

When I saw Tiff and Shalynda get out of the passenger side of Tim's car I just looked at D and quietly laughed. I can't front, a little bit of hate tried to enter me as I thought about how everybody else is getting ménages with them and I still ain't even get to watch the fucking tape.

Once the 3 of them walked up the long walkway to the front door me and D came running out of the bushes and up on them before they even heard us.

I waved my Chopper back and forth at Tiff and Shalynda. "I'll kill y'all bitches if y'all scream." I said.

Tiff and Shalynda looked like they wanted to scream but saw the devil in my eyes, so they just held each other instead.

D-Slug already had his Chopper in Tim's back.

"Open the fuckin door, Timmy." D-Slug said in a disguised voice.

Tim didn't attempt to turn around.

"Do y'all niggas know who the fuck y'all tryin to rob?" Tim asked calmly, sounding a little bit like Shaq.

"Nigga, that's why the fuck we robbin ya bitch ass. Now open the fuckin door before I open ya fuckin mellon." D-Shag replied in a disguised voice, as he rested the barrel of his burner on the back of Tim's head.

Tim ain't stupid, I thought once he stopped fumbling with the keys and unlocked the door.

Soon as Tim and D stepped in the crib, I pushed the hoes in behind them. I expected to see all types of stuntastic shit, but I was wrong. Everything in Tim's crib was average. Either this is just Tim's duck off crib or he's good as fuck at not blowing his money. I hope this is the right spot.

"Take him to the safe, cuz. I'm a stay with these bitches and get to know em a lil bit." I said and ushered Tiff and Shalynda into the living room.

D-Slug softly hit Tim in the back of his head with the barrel of his Chopper. "Let's go, nigga," he said in his disguised voice.

I caught on that D was worried that Tiff and Shalynda might recognize his voice. I was standing there with my burner aimed at the hoes in their matching miniskirts and tube tops. I started thinking about how I had to run through them before I officially hang up my player card. My thoughts were interrupted by a burst of shots.

"Cuz, you cool?" I hollered upstairs, knowing that the shots I heard were Chopper shots.

"Fuck 'good'! Nigga, we're grrreat!" D-Slug said like Tony the tiger and continued, "I'll be down in a second."

D was so excited that he had forgot to use his disguised voice.

As soon as he got done talking, I peeped Tiff nudge Shalynda with her elbow. I don't know if I was trippin or not, but I swear I heard Tiff whisper, "That's D-Slug."

I just looked at them for a long second and said, *"Now I'll never get my ménage."* Then I riddled both of their bodies with Chopper bullets.

D-Slug ran downstairs with 2 stuffed pillowcases. He took one look at the hoes and then at me.

"What the fuck, cuz?" D-Slug asked and looked back at them.

"Nigga, those hoes recognized ya voice. I rather em talk to Jesus than to them mufuckin people. Feel me?" I asked rhetorically as I grabbed him by the arm and led him out of the crib.

We ran straight to the ride and smashed off.

Once we were a good distance away from the crime

scene D looked at me with a sad face.

"Damn, JD. I'm gonna miss em," D-Slug said seriously.

"Nigga, at least you got to have a ménage with em. And I still ain't get to see the tape." I said clearly more upset than him about the way things turned out.

D-Slug knew that I had a point and that made him quickly forget about the 2 freaks that he was just sad about 2 seconds before. This nigga's crazy. I thought.

"I got it at the cut crib." He said and paused for a second, thinking about the tape. "But wait till you see what that nigga had in the safes. Yeah, I said safes. Plural, nigga." D-Slug said excitedly.

That was all that I needed to hear. I turned Lyfe on and grabbed my bottle of vodka. The rest of the drive to me and Laneisha's crib was in fast-forward as I wondered how much shit Tim had stashed.

Laneisha and Mia were both in the living room asleep on the couches, with a "paid program" for Bow Flex on the TV. Me and D tiptoed into the guestroom so that we wouldn't wake them up.

We both dumped a pillowcase on the bed at the same time. I swear it took everything inside of me to control my excitement and not wake up our women.

I grabbed D-Slug by his shoulders.

"It's on and smackin for real now, D. Fuck any nigga that ain't gonna cop off us," I whispered.

"Hell yeah, nigga. That mufucka was the fuckin Columbian port and PNC bank." D-Slug said, picking up a stack of hundred-dollar bills.

We got Tim Murphy for 17 birds of coke and $263,800. *This is it,* I thought as I continued to just stare at the prize.

"D, we eatin, chewin, and all that shit." I said once we were finished counting.

"Nigga, we digestin and shittin," D-Slug responded.

We counted the money, then put some in the flip fee and some went into the lawyer fee.

D-Slug looked at the door. "I can't believe they slept through the sound of money getting counted." He joked.

"Yo, how much you want me to put up for you?"

"Here," D-Slug said and scooted a pile of money to my side of the bed. "Put seventy-five in the piggy bank for me, cuz."

I put his $75,000 and $70,000 of mine in between the mattress in me and Laneisha's room with the rest of our stash.

"D, I'm gettin a safe first thing in the morning before I dipped out to Kiaville." I said as I walked back into the guestroom.

"I got to come out there Wednesday morning to move into my spot. My furniture and shit are supposed to be gettin dropped off that afternoon."

"Just make sure Mia don't know bout my crib out there. I still ain't figure out how I'm a break this shit down to Laneisha. I'm definitely not breakin it down to Kia," I said and thought about that old Christopher Bender song.

(Didn't one of the women kill him?)

"I don't know, JD. You and Laneisha might rumble after you tell her bout Kia's Benz." D-Slug responded and laughed.

I waited a couple of seconds before I spoke to make sure that D didn't wake up Laneisha and Mia. "I'm a leave that part out for now, but she really can't get mad, cause me and Laneisha ain't a couple. We're just us. I can't even explain this shit, cuz. I don't want to hurt her though."

"Aight, sucka for love ass nigga." D-Slug said and yawned. "I'm a stay here for the night."

I went into the living room and carried Laneisha into

our bedroom and went to sleep holding her, thinking about how to word this shit to her.

The next morning, Laneisha cooked all 4 of us breakfast before it was time to take her to school. I felt like I had to let Laneisha know the situation right now, so I stood up while everybody was still eating and headed to our bedroom.

"Baby, let me holla at you in the room real quick." I looked at Laneisha and said.

"What's up, Jakill?" She asked, closing the door behind her.

I sat on the edge of the bed and pulled her to me, so that she was standing directly in front of me. "Listen, I gotta keep it all the way funky with you bout shit. It will hurt you worse if I don't. I got.-" I was saying until she cut me off.

"Look, Jakill you don't even have to say it. I'm not slow, baby. I know you have a chick up I.U.P. and you probably have a spot with her too. Don't ask me how I know. I just know."

I immediately thought that Mia must have used her magical pussy and head powers to get D-Slug to slip up or some shit.

Laneisha continued, "I also know that you love me. But I can't say anything about girly because we never established what we are and plus she was there first. I'm not that naive. Come on, Jakill. What, was you just going to keep going out of town, without D, to a place where you can't use cell phones?" she asked and laughed.

Laneisha shocked the shit out of me to the point that I was speechless.

"Just make sure that she doesn't come around here and I'm cool, baby."

"Aight." Is all that I could manage to say.

She gave me a quick kiss and we walked out of the room.

I sat at the table while they finished eating, thinking about how mad I am that I was up all night putting together a perfect speech and I didn't even get to use it.

Once we all got ourselves together, D and Mia went on their way, and me and Laneisha drove to Westinghouse.

"Baby, I got to go on a trip for the next few nights, but I'll be here in the afternoon to pick you up from school every day." I said awkwardly.

I knew that it would be easy to manage because Kia has afternoon classes.

"I love you, Jakill," she said as we pulled up at her school and she was getting out of the car.

"Oh, yeah, call and schedule a time to take ya driving test for this Saturday. And I love you too, Neisha Boo." I said and pulled off.

As I was driving away from the school, I just happened to pull up on the side of Daz in his mom's car that D-Slug must have let him get. Daz put his window down to say what's up and that's when I noticed that Chanel was in the passenger seat.

"What's up, JD?" Daz asked as he leaned out of the window.

Chanel was sticking up her middle finger at me where Daz couldn't see it.

"Ain't shit. I see you got you a dime in the ride with you." I said to stroke his ego and not make him feel awkward.

I never been a hater!

"Yeah. This Chanel. She's from the hood."

"I don't know her."

She looked over at me, surprised that I played it like that.

"I'm a get at you on the block in a couple days cause

I'm dippin out of town again. Holla at cuz if you need somethin." I said and smashed off, thinking about how that probably got Chanel tweakin to get at me again.

CHAPTER 16

I drove to this spot out Lawrenceville and bought 2 big ass safes for my crib with Laneisha. As usual I paid extra cause I'm an impatient nigga. I got them to deliver and install them in the next hour. I got one of them in the closet in each bedroom.

Once the workers were out of my crib, I put the 21 birds of powder in the guestroom safe. The safe in our bedroom was filled with the crack, flip fee, D's stash, and exactly half of my stash. I put the other half of my stash and the lawyer fee in my duffle bag and sat it on my bed.

I went to lay back on the bed for a second to relax before I hit the road but J-Meanmug stopped that.

"Got my mind right and the Chopper held tight/ Nigga let me know wutz smackin 2night."

I looked at the Caller ID. "What's smackin, Mayo?"

"Ready for a quarter-pounder with cheese real, quick, and Big Hurt want a six piece of extra crispy. I ain't seen nobody else yet. I been doin me, cuz," Mayo said and placed an order for him and Hurt.

MORE BIRDS MORE BODIES

"I definitely feel you. I'll be at the spot in like fifteen, cuz." I said and hung up.

As soon as I hung up with Mayo, Kia called.

"Hey, daddy." Kia said seductively and instantly made my dick get hard.

"What's up, sexy?"

"Missing you. The usual."

"I'm missing you too. You already know. I'm finishin up business right now, so I'll be home round five-somethin. Let me get back to this and I'll see you then. Aight?"

"Alright, daddy. I'll be waiting covered in ice cream." She said and giggled.

After we hung up, I sat there and thought about Kia's sexy ass in nothing but ice cream until for some reason I remembered that I was supposed to holla at Drizzy a couple hours ago.

I called Keva's crib, not caring if he wondered how I got her number.

"Yo, who this?" Drizzy answered the phone sounding like the killer that I knew he wasn't.

"This JD, cuz. Meet me in the back of ya spot in a couple minutes."

"Got you!" He responds, and we hung up.

I went into the crack safe, using the digital code that I remembered that quick, and weighed up 9 zips, 6 zips, and 1 zip. Then I put it all in my duffle bag with the money. I put the rest of the crack back in the safe, grabbed the bag, and dipped.

I got in my car and took the single ounce out of the bag. Then I put the bag on the floor in the back and then pulled off. On the way around the corner to meet Drizzy I thought about sending S a $10,000 money order just to shock him, but then I changed my mind because that would be the same as handcuffing me and my brother for them motherfuckers. So, I decided on flying him another stack and going to visit him next weekend, even though he don't really like visits.

I pulled up on Drizzy, who was looking grimy in dirty fatigues, and told him to hop in. That look made me get on my paranoid shit for a second and I was mad that my Chopper was in the trunk, but then I remembered that it was only Drizzy.

"Cuz, listen." I said once he got in and I broke down the same deal that I gave my block niggas.

I thought I saw him eyehustling everything in my

car, but I chalked it up as that paranoid shit still lingering.

After he agreed with the terms, I gave him the zip, gave him a pound, and dipped to the cut crib. I drove to the block thinking about how Drizzy's body language and eyehustling was bothering me a little bit, but since it was only Drizzy I chalked it up to me on my paranoid shit again.

I pulled up on the block to only see Mayo and Big Hurt out. I guess niggas is still on some low-key shit cause of the drama that has been going on. For that reason, I only planned on dropping off the work and getting the fuck from on the block. I'm tired of getting locked up. plus, this is the longest run I ever had and I'm not trying to fuck this up right now. I thought as I got out of my car.

Mayo stood there in a new big ass Gucci link with a big ass money bag medallion on it. "Damn, cuz, I could of, flipped a whole extra value meal by now," he said while pulling out stacks of money from his pockets.

"And supersized it." Big Hurt added and started going in his pockets too.

These niggas are getting ready to get us booked, I thought, but still took the money out of their hands in the open.

I served them the work right out of my car instead of taking them into the cut crib. I figured that it was cool since it was only a quick transaction and I already had the work in separate baggies.

"Yo, I'm a get at y'all niggas later." I said and started my car up.

"Aight, cuz," Mayo said and went through the cut on the side of the cut crib.

"I'll holla later, cuz," Big Hurt said and began to walk towards the porch steps. He took 3 steps and then quickly turned around. Then he put his finger in the air to tell me to hold up because I had just turned on my sounds and couldn't hear what he was trying to say.

"Oh, yeah," Big Hurt said once I turned off the Jadakiss CD. "The Homi detectives was walkin round yesterday bout Nut and Wokky, but I ain't peep no mufuckas rappin to em."

"Who was they?" I asked hoping that the detectives weren't those dirty ass motherfuckers, David Lucas and Reggy Kravits.

David Lucas is known as "The Confessor" because he allegedly can make anyone confess to their crimes. Even the Pittsburgh Post Gazzette newspaper done an article about him that was 5 pages long. The truth is, like most of us hood niggas know already, that David Lucas doesn't get anyone to confess to shit. He'll either straight up lie on you or trick a slow motherfucker into confessing to somebody else's crime. He's so good with his shit that he'll fold a piece of paper 3 times, have you written on it that you didn't have anything to do with the crime and sign it. Once you sign it, that's your ass because he will unfold the paper and write on the other 2 folds how you told him that you done the crime and how sorry you are, but the way it was folded puts your signature right under where he writes at, so it looks official. The worse one was when some niggas shot up a police station and he told one of the niggas that the pigs said that they'll drop charges if he signs an "apology letter."

The letter said,

"Dear Mr. Officer, I'm sorry for shooting up your police station and I'm sorry that one of the bullets hit you in your foot. If I could go back in time, I wouldn't have shot up your police station. I accept full responsibility for my half of the crime, and I hope that my co-defendant can accept responsibility for his role. Please accept my apology. Sincerely...." That was an open and shut case for both of them, even though his co-defendant was smarter than him and didn't sign anything, but David Lucas lied on him anyway.

Reggy Kravits used to be the worse homicide detective until Lucas passed him up. Now Kravits just rides with Lucas on everything. The 2 differences between them are that Kravits will also plant a dirty burner on you, and he will also say that he saw you flash a gun and that's why he shot you before he plants that gun on you.

Hurt shook his head. "Lucas and Kravits." He replied.

Them pigs is probably framing somebody right now for those bodies, or else making a dumb motherfucker confess to that shit even though he ain't do it, I thought as I sped away from the block.

CHAPTER 17

Everything has been good for me and D-Slug for the past 10 months now. We are no longer just Homiwood, Hale Street niggas. We're now officially 2 of The Burgh's Big Niggas. It's crazy that we're young as fuck but still be mentioned in the same breath as the big nigga, Pager, from the Hill District and the big nigga, Cheeks, from the North Side. I never would have imagined that I would be sitting like this one day.

Boo and Mayo are right with us eating. The rest of The Tre is butt. I'll get to them in a second.

Me, D-Slug, Boo, and Mayo was the squad. We were living it up in different ways, but when my birthday came, we all, even Boo, were on some ultimate stuntin shit. The 4 of us and our women (I had Kia and Laneisha there) threw me a big ass party on the Gateway Clipper Fleet boat. It was Gators and suits for niggas and Stilettos and dresses for women. That motherfucker was so live that I even had J-Meanmug, Dub, G-Money, Smamez Loc, and some new young nigga, Lil Brucie, all on the stage at the same time doing an exclusive song that all of them spit on.

There were niggas from every hood there, niggas that was eating, and even some niggas that were broke but looked like they were eating for the night. Everything was on the house, so nobody had to pay for shit, not even the bottle of Crystal, Dom P, or Moet. Niggas actually all got along... until the party was over and all these niggas from different hoods were in the parking lot where their burners were.

One Wilkinsburg nigga got slumped and 2 Hill niggas got hit on some minor shit. I was just glad that nothing happened during my party, because I made sure that I was the only one on the boat with a burner. I knew that since there was so much money on that boat, I had to be on point 300% more than usual. When it was all said and done, everybody said that my party was better than Scooter and C. Knowles' cookout party at Frick Park in 2000—and that was one of the livest parties ever!

I had also ended up getting a hold of my dad's brother, Uncle Craig. He was still posted up down Richmond, Virginia. After we argued for a while about why I didn't get down with him a minute ago when he had first asked me to, Unc put me on to them thangs for only

$13,500 a byrd. Plus, they got dropped off to us by different bad ass broads, only because we were Hipping so much weight and Unc wanted to stunt on us. I knew Unc was getting money but when he had initially said "$13,500" I thought he was bullshitting so I bullshitted him for 2 weeks until D-Slug had finally talked me into driving down there to see if he was on some real shit and, if not, we planned on jacking him.

Me and D are getting off 20 birds a week in just quarter birds and eighths of birds. Plus, we were running through 25 birds a week just by copping them for $13,500 and then selling them to niggas for $22,000.

Mayo is fucking with 15 birds a week throughout the Eastside. That really surprised me. Boo is handling 20 birds a week out Altoona, PA. That's no real surprise there.

D-Slug had put 3 safes in his crib with Mia and he don't be blowing his money anymore like he used to. I still can't believe that he knocked Mia's ass up. She's 8 months pregnant. They also are faithful to each other that made me believe in miracles—and they are together anywhere that you see them.

On that note, yeah, Kia and Laneisha are both 5½ months pregnant. I still can't understand how they both got knocked up at the same time. That shit had broken up me and Kia for like 3 days when I told her, but she just had to accept it like the rider that I knew that she was. Kia was still my #1 even though I spend more time with Laneisha. Laneisha even surprised me by getting my name tattooed on her neck, thigh, and the small of her back.

I'm getting Laneisha a spot out Penn Hills next week. The crazy thing about that is that the crib that I'm getting her is Jeff Rose's old crib. It's paid for in cash already. I knew that I would get that crib one day. As of right now she's still staying at the apartment on The Ave. It took me all of this time to talk her into moving. There weren't any niggas dumb enough to try running up on me or in my crib, but I rather be safe than sorry with the ones I love. Plus, I still keep a little bit of work there for when I'm on some lazy shit and somebody on the Ave. might want to cop something, so I'll just grab it and run around back real quick.

We got a new cut crib on the block where I keep most of the work. I don't ever worry about somebody trying to rob the spot because like I said, ain't no niggas dumb enough to try it, and we got a team of young headbustas guarding it.

The young niggas are called The Hale Street HB's (Headbustas). There are 5 of them. Daz's little bother, Lil Slug, who was only just turning 14 years old. Gizzle's little brother, C-Blacc, and their homies, Moo, Blue, and UC (Ugly Cuz).

The oldest HB is only 16 years old, but they are way ahead of their time. These niggas just came off of the porch within the past 6 months and already put in more work than most niggas older than me. 1 had them take care of a few roadblocks that were in me and D's way. Now they all are getting money just by posting up on the block, guarding the fort, and taking care of anything that gets in our way. I swear them little niggas be praying that somebody tries some shit just, so they can bust a nigga's head. They all even got the Hale Street Devil tattooed on their right arms like the rest of us, but they have all of the HB's names under it and all of The Tre niggas' names going around it, with a "X" through Big Hurt's name and E-Wok's name. That's how thorough them niggas are. I love them crazy motherfuckers!

I still push the Iroc Z every now and then but I'm usually in my new black on black Caddy CTS. D-Slug grabbed up the black STS, but he still pushes his 5.0 more than anything else. To show that we were the Big Niggas we both copped matching Chrysler 300's and got them painted royal blue before we even drove them. Laneisha only wanted a fucking Neon but I forced her into a brand-new champagne Lexus GS300. I upgraded Kia's Benz to a platinum SL500 (that's when she forgave me for a double life). D copped Mia the new cherry red Lexus ES350.

The smartest nigga might be Boo though. He was low key, riding in a new Chevy Malibu with factory rims and tinted windows. His car still got the factory sounds in it. And he lives in a regular apartment in Monroeville with his BM. You wouldn't even think that Boo was eating like he is by his look and lifestyle. The only time that I remember seeing him with any ice on was at my party, and it still wasn't anything too heavy. A nigga would see Boo and think that he was a regular nigga on maybe 4½ zips.

Mayo on the other hand is known as a stunta. He even changed his name to The Mayor because he runs the East Side of The Burgh hands down. His stuntin is almost up there with Baby from Cash Money Records. Mayo switches cars every month. You might see him in a brand-new Corvette today and next month he'll be in a brand-new Jaguar. That's not including the fact that he has a brand-new drop top Bentley Continental GT, that he got painted all white with a royal blue devil chasing a money bag with feet around the car. He also had twin yellow SS Monte Carlo's. It's crazy though because he's eating and stuntin and still living in the hood. He bought his mom a crib in Stanton Heights, where he keeps his cars at, but him and 2 of his 5 BM's stay together in a row house on Cora Street.

Niggas won't try him out of fear of our squad and because, he's respected more than even I am. That respect comes from the fact that he single handedly put together a Homiwood basketball league with inner leagues for niggas in different age groups. Believe it or not but that slowed down some of the violence in the hood. Once that league blew up, he, merged with the Hill nigga, Pager, and the North Side nigga, Cheeks, to form "The Steel City Hood League." All The Burgh's hoods played against each other and not even one shoot-out ever occurs at the games. Mayo's team wins every game though because he has the best team and Pitt's 2 new recruits.

guards, Bug and Dell. Me and D be winning $5,000 a game on Mayo's team, some niggas lose more than that. I'm just glad that Mayo found a way to continue his basketball dream and make a way for kids to perfect their game in his "Lil Nigga League."

Teeke had got grabbed for questioning about the deaths of Walnut and E-Wok 2 weeks after that shit went down because some smoker told about the day, he was bustin back at Walnut's ride with the Chopper, so the homi's figured that he probably finished the job. Lucas and Kravits got his dumb ass to say that he slumped Walnut over a debt, and he killed E-Wok so that he won't snitch. TK even signed a letter that Lucas addressed to E-Wok's mom. He's looking at an automatic Life Sentence. I keep his books right though on the strength that no matter what he's still from The Tre because he didn't snitch and took his fuck up on the chin, and because I don't want him to get the idea to snitch. Plus, I'm a real nigga!

My little nigga, Daz, got killed 3 months ago when a nigga tried to rob him at Chanel's crib. Me and D-Slug personally went with the HB's to ride for that, but Lil Slug wouldn't let anybody but him shoot the nigga who was responsible for killing his brother once we found him. Lil Slug had stuck his 45 in Big Hurt's mouth and busted the entire clip. Then he put 3 one-dollar bills on Big Hurt's chest to honor his brother. Now all The Tre niggas and HB's have "R.I.P. DAZ" and a picture of him tattooed on our left shoulders.

The Feds grabbed Gizzle last month. He had a spot out by St. Francis College. It was bangin out there, but he got too reckless. Gizzle had sold a byrd straight to the Feds and when they ran up in his crib, they found the 3 Choppers that me and D-Slug gave him after we told him that they were dirty. I also found out that he was getting high off of dope. That hurt me, but I can't knock the next man's high.

The nigga, Drizzy .... What can I say? I guess some niggas was born to be broke. He had copped a zip off of me once and came back 2 days later trying to cop 7 fucking grams. I cut him off ASAP. Keva told me that Drizzy felt some type of way about me cutting him off that quick but since he wasn't anybody to worry about, I didn't pay that any attention.

I did pay Keva some attention though. I knocked her off once or twice for old time sake (raw dog as usual). Don't get me wrong, she got a good shot, but I realized that I had thought that her pussy was so unbelievable only because when me and her was fucking back then I wasn't really getting too much of any other pussy to compare it to. We're still cool as fuck and I make sure that her and Pooh are cool. Like I said earlier, don't ask, don't tell.

I never got to see the tape of Tiff and Shalynda because allegedly it got stolen out of the cut crib. I even went to the extent of putting out a $5,000 reward for whoever found that tape, but it never was found. I thought that D might have been lying on his dick until he added $10,000 to the reward because he said that the tape was the only thing left of Tiff and Shalynda that he had. That made me tweak to see the tape more because I figured that they must be able to do some freaky shit to have this nigga's nose wide open like that. The tape will probably pop up on Youtube one day or some shit.

As for Lil Erny, that leads me to today ....

CHAPTER 18

I had only talked to Lil Erny twice in like the past 4 months. Once when I bought a Desert Eagle and another time when I bought an AR-15. That was due to the fact that his gun connect had got booked down North Carolina. The word was that Lil Erny was struggling so I tried to talk him into getting on the squad and slangin work. I even offered to front him 2 birds just because he always preaches about how family is supposed to stick together and look out for each other. I don't know if it was his pride, the fact that I'm younger than him, or both, but he quickly turned down my offer and acted like he had found a new gun connect. What got me was that I had invited him to my birthday party, but he didn't even show up.

Now here I am at me and Laneisha's spot beating up her pussy when Lil Erny calls my house phone.

"Cuz, I got a Tommy and two grenades." Lil Erny said.

"Yo, you serious?" I asked excitedly forgetting that I'm breaking my "no business on the crib phone" rule.

"Hell, yeah! I'm serious, nigga."

He must have really found a new connect and I like this one better already. I thought. I jumped on that immediately. "I'll meet you down Fleury in like five minutes." I said while putting on a pair of shorts without even putting on my boxers.

"I'm riding down The Ave right now. I'll just stop at ya spot." He replied.

I never do any business at me and Laneisha's crib unless it's with D-Slug but I'm tweakin for that Tommy Gun and grenades, plus we're moving out next week anyway. It won't hurt to break another rule, I decided.

"Aight, but hurry up, cuz."

Not even 2 minutes later there was a knock at the door. He must have known that I wouldn't turn down this purchase, I thought as I grabbed $5,000 out of the safe in our bedroom.

"Baby, that's Lil Erny at the door. Let me handle this business real quick." I said and watched her give me a crazy look for breaking my own rule. I continued, "I know, but don't worry. It's cool. And don't put no clothes on either cause I ain't done wearing out that pregnant pussy."

"Hurry up back, Jakill. And you better not leave,"

Laneisha said and quickly opened and shut her legs to give me a glance and tease me.

I walked through the hallway while the knocking got louder. "Here I come, cuz." I hollered.

I got to the door and got a strange feeling but I ignored it.

"So, what's this shit costing me." I said as I opened the door.

Boom!

I couldn't even react fast enough when I saw the burner. One bullet hit me in my right thigh. It made me stumble back a couple feet but didn't really hurt like I thought being shot would. I hope it didn't hit that artery, I thought as blood ran down my leg.

The Glock raised up and was pressed to my forehead.

I hope Laneisha dip down the fire escape or something.

"The next one gonna be ya potato, nigga. Now let's get that coke and cheddar, baller." Drizzy said while standing next to Lil Erny, who was aiming a 40 cal at me.

"Erny, what the fuck this nigga talked you into?" I asked Lil Erny confused, not believing that my own family would try to rob me.

How could Lil Erny always talk that family shit and then try this. I can remember all the times that he had talked that shit. When me and D-Slug first found out that we were family and rumbled on the block. When he killed the snitch nigga, Dre, after I shot Black. When S first got booked and he gave me some money to send him. When I bought the Choppers off of him and all those times had just flashed through my head.

Lil Erny looked at me and grinned. "You mean, what did I talk him into. Nigga show me the fuckin money." He said and pushed me backwards.

I hope Laneisha dipped down the fire escape or something.

"Aight! Aight! The safe's in the guestroom closet," I said hoping that they just take this $5,000 in my pocket and the 10 birds that I left down here in the safe, and not look for the rest of the money so that they won't find Laneisha if she didn't make it out of the crib.

I had already noticed that they didn't have on any masks, so I knew that they were planning on killing me and anybody else who is in the crib with me. I'm sure that they knew damn well that if they didn't kill me, I would murder everybody who even knows them.

I limped to the guestroom with Lil Erny and Drizzy on my heels aiming guns at the back of me. My mind was racing trying to figure out how the fuck I'm going to get out of this situation, and how I'm going to make sure that my woman makes it out of this situation as well. I was thinking so much that I no longer felt the slightest pain from my leg shot as I knelt in the closet to open the safe.

"Hurry the fuck up, bitch ass nigga." Drizzy ordered me.

I guess he caught on to my stalling tactics.

"Aight, cuz, be easy." I replied still trying to stall long enough to figure something out.

I hope Laneisha dipped down the fire escape or something.

I knew right then and there that my only option was my backup plan that I already knew would never work in a million years.

It's now or never. I thought as I finished putting in the combination. As soon as I pulled the lever to open the safe, I heard a single gunshot. I was expecting to feel a quick jolt in my head before I died or some shit like that, but I felt nothing.

It was like everything was in slow motion as I turned around and saw the nigga, Drizzy's, lifeless body hit the floor. Lil Erny started turning around late. I was too confused right then to process that quick what happened, so instead of trying too, I used Lil Erny's late reaction as the split second that I needed.

I quickly reached in the safe and grabbed the Glock 40 that I had put in there as just an inside joke type of thing.

Lil Erny was now raising his burner to aim at the doorway. I don't know how I was quicker on the draw, but I spit 3 shots out before he even pulled his trigger. Lil Erny fell face first with his last thought all over the wall and carpet.

I guess that burner in the safe shit do work sometimes. I thought and smiled.

That was too close for comfort. I'm just glad D-Slug got here when he did. I thought as I finally looked through the doorway assuming D had just happened to show up at the right time.

I couldn't believe my eyes. I was staring at Laneisha naked holding a 380 that I had bought her. I still was half expecting to see D standing on the side of her.

I still remember when I bought her the gun for protection a few months ago. "Get it away from me. I don't like guns." She had said and forced me to put it in a box in the back of our bedroom closet. Now she's standing there like Bonnie or Ma Barker or somebody.

Laneisha ran over to me and knelt on the floor next to me. She wasn't crying or shaking or any of that shit that you would expect a woman to do in a situation like this.

Kia would never have stuck around to ride for me. I thought. It was at that very moment that I realized that I was wrong all this time about which one of the two was the real rider.

She softly put her hands on my face and gave me a quick peck on my lips while we stared in each other's eyes.

"I love you, Neisha Boo." I finally said after a moment of silence.

"I love you too, Jakill. Enough to kill for you." Laneisha said seriously.

I immediately went into lawyer mode.

I grabbed the 380 that Laneisha was still holding.

"Baby, we got to get everything out of here before the pigs show up." I said and started dumping the pillows out of the pillowcases. "Take one of these and put all of the money from the other safe in it. I'm a grab this." I began emptying the safe.

Laneisha took the pillowcase out of my hand and ran out of the room without saying a word. She came running back in the guestroom in less than a minute with the pillowcase full of cash and still naked.

I gave her the pillowcase that I had just filled with the work from the guestroom closet. "Take this shit to D's crib and stay there. I need you to call Kia." I said and watched her frown her face up. "Tell her I'm in jail and to call my lawyers cause she already got the lawyer scrilla and their numbers. Don't worry, baby, I got this. I'll call you when I hit intake. And one more thing."

"What's that, Jakill?"

I lifted her left leg and licked her pussy one quick time. "That should hold us over for a minute. Now put ya clothes on and get out of here fast before the pigs get here."

The pigs ended up arriving right after Laneisha pulled off. They took me to the hospital and had me handcuffed and shackled to the bed. I wasn't there long because the bullet had gone clean though. I just got patched up like an old bike innertube and then they took me to the homicide station in Point Breeze, knowing that I'm 300% coded. I guess they had time to waste.

The regular pigs put me in a small boxed-in interview room and shackled me to a ring that was bolted to the floor. Then they left me in there alone to wait for the homi-detectives to start their bullshit.

I was sitting there thinking about how Laneisha just showed me thoroughness that I didn't even know that a woman could possess. I owe her everything.

Lucas and Kravits walked in the room and slammed the door as hard as possible to snap me out of my half sleep daze.

Lucas sat down in the chair next to me and scooted it around so that it faced me.

"So, we finally meet, Mr. Freeman. Would you care to inform us what happened at your drug house tonight?" Lucas asked with his coffee breath directly in my face.

I smiled at him. "Wymardine!" I said.

Lucas acted like he didn't hear what I had said, "Why did you kill those guys?" He asked.

"Diffon!" I replied.

Kravits walked from around the table and stood on the other side of me. "Was it a drug deal gone bad?"

Kravits asked.

I looked at the ceiling, shook my head looked at Kravits and smiled at him, then said, "Foglias."

Lucas changed his tone thinking that he could scare me. "Look here you little drug dealing, fake player, wanna-be gangster. We're not gonna sit here and bullshit around with you."

"We know you killed them. But what I can't figure out is how both of them got shot in the back on their heads at different directions and you had two guns on you that were discharged, but only one shell spent from the three-eighty and three spent from the dock." Kravitz said in a soft tone.

I guess he's the good cop. I thought and smiled.

"Why switch guns in the middle of a fucking shoot-out?" Lucas asked and grabbed the arm rests of the chair that I was sitting in.

I looked at Lucas and then at Kravits and smiled again. "Anybody but that weak mufucka. Houdarr!" I said and laughed.

I sat in that interview room for 3 hours straight just naming different lawyers' names until I ran out of names and just started making up names that sounded like lawyers. I was just wasting time until my 2 lawyers, William Kaczynski and Michael Kalocay, got there but they never showed up.

The detectives got frustrated and even attempted to send a couple rookies in to question me like they might have had a better angle. They ended up all getting tired of me naming lawyers, which I now started rhyming with the next name, and tired of violating my rights, so they took me to get arraigned and then to the Allegheny County Jail.

Once in the jail I got my mugshot taken, fingerprinted and then sent to the back intake holding room where the phones and vending machines are. They were trying to rush me through the process because that room is usually just for people that can get out on bond, so they let them sit there and try to get out instead of wasting time and paper by putting them on a pod for just a few hours. I gave the black woman that was in control of processing $100 to let me rock out there for a minute while I make calls and eat for a little bit.

I bought a bag of chips, a Pepsi, and then ran to a phone to call D-Slug's crib.

Laneisha answered on the 1st ring. "Baby, please be you." She desperately said.

"Yeah, it's me, Neisha Boo. I just touched I take finally. What's good with that lawyer situation though cause they ain't come through the homi spot?" I asked expecting her to tell me that they're on the way or some shit.

She took a deep breath. "Baby, I called Kia and that bitch talking about 'fuck you that's what you get,' and 'he ain't gettin that money'. Jakill, I swear if we weren't both pregnant, I would go beat that bitch's ass."

I rolled with the punches. "Don't worry bout that bitch. We got more money than that bitch can count. Here's my lawyers' numbers." I said and waited for her to get a pen and then gave her the information. "I want you to stay at D and Mia's crib and I'm a call you first thing in the morning. Holla at my lawyers, baby. I love you, Neisha Boo. Put D on the phone."

She sniffled and finally let out those built up tears. "I love you too, Jakill. I promise I'll make sure that your lawyers holla at you. I love you, baby." She said and then handed D-Slug the phone.

"Cuz, who got to get it to get you out?" D-Slug asked seriously like our call wasn't being monitored.

Ain't too many niggas that would ride at all cost like

I knew D would. I thought. "Nobody, cuz. I'm gonna beat those bodies cause it's obvious what went down. I'm a have to take the two guns on the chin. That ain't bout shit though. But they definitely ain't givin me a bail, so hold it down. Go past the cut crib ASAP and make sure the HB's know ya still stompin so don't no, funny shit jump off." I said.

"Anything else, cuz?"

"Yeah. Since I'm a be sittin for a minute make sure you hit S off with a stack every Friday, and I need you to toss Keva a stack every Friday too, D."

"Nigga!" D-Slug said in a hushed voice and continued, "ol boy just tried to slump you and you want me to give his fuckin BM scrilla. It can't be that good, JD. I mean ... oh shit! I don't know how the fuck I never caught on." D-Slug said and paused for a second. "Why ain't you ever put me down?"

I shook my head. *Don't ask, don't tell. It's just a more fucked up mess now.* I said and had to wait for the woman officer to finish telling me that her sergeant was on her heels about a "homicide inmate" being in intake longer than 10 minutes so I had to shoot upstairs to a pod in a few minutes.

"Yo, this CO bitch just conned me out of a buck. But look, I'm bout to go upstairs, cuz. I need you to watch out for my girl, D. She's gonna hold it down for me till I touch. I'm a get at you tomorrow."

"Stay up, JD."

CHAPTER 19

It's been 2½ years since I first came to the county jail on this bullshit. I been on the homicide pod (8D) the entire time. Teeke was on the same pod as me until 6 months ago when he took a plea for second 3rd Degree murders and got two 10-20-year bits running together. He came up under the circumstances even though he had nothing to do with either of them bodies. Now he's at Dallas Penitentiary out east somewhere. There was 2 other Homiwood niggas on the pod for a minute but they were on their appeals, so they went back up state. I didn't have anything to worry about anyway.

The whole time I been here I been "That Nigga" just like on the street. D-Slug had one of his old freaks bringing me dro on visits. I don't smoke weed still and don't really need the money, but I was just doing it because I miss the hustle and other niggas had regular weed and I wanted to shit on them by keeping a constant supply of that good shit. Me and TK had even run up in some nigga's cell and took his commissary just because he said some slick shit out of his mouth to TK, plus, I was missing the feeling I used to get from jacking niggas.

My only fight happened a month ago. A Hill nigga named Poe tried me I guess because he thought that I needed niggas to back me up and they were gone. He gave me a good rumble at 1st but I ended up beating the brakes off of him and set an example. Other niggas be fighting every other day and there's a stabbing at least once a week somewhere in the jail.

What fucked me up is that every hood has its own phone. I quickly put my claim on 8D as a whole.

My nigga, Gizzle started out on 6F where the certified juveniles were at, but he been on his "me against the world" complex and been wilding out on CO's and other niggas. That nigga was going crazy. Everytime he went to the hole he has to walk past my pod, and he be throwing up The Tre sign every time. The Feds are trying to get him to take a 7½-15 years plea in a state pen since he's young and, believe it or not, this is his 1st charge ever.

Laneisha moved into Jeff Rose's crib and had my daughter, Jakia Destiny Freeman. They come visit me twice a week every week. My little girl looks just like her mother. Also, Laneisha attends Pitt so she could get some degrees in business. She plans on taking some change and opening up a couple of beauty shops and clothing spots in The Burgh, so she needs those credentials.

Kia had my son, Jakill Jr., or Lil JD as I call him. If he didn't look like a spitting image of me, I would try to get a DNA test done because I found out exactly how foul that bitch really is. Right after she gave birth to my son, she took him and moved to Atlanta, in a house that my lawyer fee paid for. I still can't believe that I thought that she was the rider. I don't even know their address. Shit, I only know what my son looks like because out of the blue she sent me 1 picture of him without a letter in the envelope and no return address, but the post stamp was from Atlanta. That bitch got me for a punk ass $100,000. If she only knew that Laneisha is holding more than a million in cash, she would kill herself. Not to mention that's not including our half of the Hip fee. Nigga, we are eating, chewing, digesting, and shitting. I swear as soon as I get out, I'm going to take my son from her, so he could live it up and not have to grow up the way that I did.

D-Slug been holding it down more than I could have ever expected. He keeps the business right and splits everything straight down the middle with Laneisha who is also the "accountant" for our business. D and Mia bought the house right down the street from Laneisha's so that they all can watch out for each other and be like family is supposed to be and not just preach it like Lil Erny did.

S will be home soon and half of mine is his. D already bought S a crib a block away from our spots and grabbed him a brand-new Yukon with zero miles on it. Plus, you already know that S has a royal blue Chrysler 300 waiting on him.

As far as me.... the DA threw out the 2 bodies for self-defense (I might be the 1st nigga that ever actually got off on self-defense), and I pleaded guilty to the 2 burners. I'm sitting in the bullpen right now about to accept the 2 ½-5 years with time served and an immediate release on parole, which means that I won't have to go upstate to see the parole board. I'm just going to have to go back to the jail for a couple hours and wait for the paperwork to go through. My 2 lawyers are the best there ARE and they earned their money.

I can't wait until I'm finally able to hold my little girl and take my son from Kia so that they can grow up together. I keep thinking about me and S finally being able to eat together. I was thinking about everything before, during, and after my plea hearing. I got to be more on point and not sleeping on niggas like how niggas was sleeping on me and D-Slug.

After my plea hearing I got back to 8D. The only thing that was on my mind was calling D-Slug and letting him know that I was getting out even though I'm sure that Laneisha called him as soon as she walked out of the courtroom.

Niggas on the pod was asking me what happened at court and all that good shit that gives niggas an ounce of hope on the homicide pod. Most of them were rooting for me because they knew that I was a real nigga with money and I had told them that if I get out I was going to put $100 on all their accounts just to stunt, and I meant it. Right now, though, my only thought was getting on the phone, so I just said, "I'm out of here today" and kept it moving without paying niggas any attention.

I heard somebody say something about some new nigga on the pod, but I was only thinking about getting on that phone. Plus, it probably wasn't important anyway. He was probably just some nigga that I served work to before trying to see if I could make something crack for him or some shit like that.

I finally reached the phone and picked it up to call D- Slug. Some new nigga with a full beard covering up most of his face like he was Muslim, a Freeway looking nigga but skinny, walked up on the side of me.

I don't know this nigga, and he must have come from a downstairs pod because ain't nobody just get grabbed for any homicides today or it would have been getting talked about in the bullpen.

"Yo, I'm on the phone. Holla at me bout whatever when I'm done." I said and turned my back to him, so he could get lost.

I felt that the nigga was still there as D's phone started ringing. *What the fuck this nigga want?* I thought and turned back around to ask him.

"Cuz, I said I'm on the phone." I said angrily.

This time I got a good look at him and something inside of me said that I know him, but I couldn't automatically put a name to his bearded face. I knew it wasn't about any drama, I thought because the nigga was so skinny, and I figured that I would beat him the fuck up without even punching him.

I turned my back on him again when D-Slug answered the phone.

"What's up, JD? I hear ya getting out in a few hours. You know we gonna do it big." D-Slug said.

"Nigga, I told all of these niggas I'm a put a buck on they, books soon as I walk out the door so bring some scrilla with you for me. You know I gotta get stuntastic off top, D," I said and felt that the nigga was still standing there. "Hold on, cuz, some weird mufucka act like I owe him or something."

I turned around and the nigga was still there. I held the phone down at my side. "Yo, cuz, do I know you or somethin?" I asked the nigga and then put on my meanmug face.

He rubbed his beard real slow. "Oh, you don't remember me?" He asked.

Where the fuck do, I know this nigga from? I wondered. "Naw, cuz, but like I said, I'm on the phone so I'll holla at you in a minute." I said and turned my back on him for the 3rd time.

"Yeah though," I said into the phone.

Before I could get out another word, I felt the cold metal enter the side of my neck. I dropped the phone and took the whack in my neck 4 more times quickly before I could even react.

I turned around and tried to grab the weird nigga that was stabbing me, but the whack was moving too fast for me to dodge all the pokes.

Where do I know this nigga from?

I was instantly weak but still was trying to fight him. I managed to get my hands around his neck for a quick second. I thought that I would be able to choke the nigga until the whack found my stomach.

Where do I know this nigga from?

It's crazy how none of these niggas is riding with me right now. I thought as I looked up and saw niggas standing on top of tables and shit. I was now down on one knee still fighting. My arms were cut up from blocking some of the pokes and I was feeling weaker and weaker as my blood puddled the floor around us. I knew this nigga wanted me dead, but I couldn't go out like no bitch, and somehow some way I got to make it out of this situation.

Where do I know this nigga from?

"Oh, you still don't remember me? I was that sweet?" He asked rhetorically while he stabbed me again in my chest.

I was trying to grab at anything but could barely hold myself up. Hang in there, cuz, I willed myself.

Where do I know this nigga from?

"You don't remember Clear Eyes gets the red out and all that shit, nigga? What, you thought I wouldn't catch you one day mufucka?" He snapped as he stabbed me in my chest one more time.

I could no longer hold on. I can't even count how many times he stabbed me but at least I left one of his eyes swollen somehow.

But where do I know this ....

As I was falling to the floor, I finally realized who this nigga is.

"I guess payback's a bitch, huh, Tizz?" I said with my last breath.

Maybe Tiff and Shalynda will let me have that ménage. I thought and died with a smile on my face.

Payback's A Bitch!
J. D. B.

Biggie once said it best, "More money, more problems!"

But Where I come from its: MORE BIRDS, MORE BODIES.

J.D.B.

I pray that my kids be alright... All 3 of them.......

THE STORY CONTINUES IN
MORE BODIES, MORE BIRDS......

"You don't get to cry for me/be back before you know it/ You don't got to cry for me/ This the life I live, I chose it/ You don't got to cry for me/ If I die, just keep it movin/ But you don't got to cry for me/ Cause sometimes the ones you love, you lose them.

J-Meanmug — *"Cry For Me"*